The scene etched itself into my mind.

Reverend Annie was standing in the darkened sanctum. She was goldenly naked, a shimmering vision of feminine beauty poised in an attitude of exultant worship with feet together and stretching upward from the toes almost like a ballerina, back arched gracefully and the chest thrown high, head back as far as it could go and the arms raised and reaching as though she were trying to project herself along that beam of light.

"You told me she was in jail," the security guard muttered.

"Last I heard, she was," I muttered back.

"God! Did you see her? Did you *see* that?"

I saw it, yeah, but I was not quite as willing to accept the evidence of the sense perceptions. An *extra*sensory quiver, back there, had me working along another thread from the loom.

I beat a path to a pay phone near the gazebo.

And, yeah, the quiver had it right. The Reverend Ann Marie Farrel was still in jail.

**The Ashton Ford novels
by Don Pendleton**

Ashes to Ashes
Eye to Eye
Mind to Mind
Life to Life
Heart to Heart*

Published by
POPULAR LIBRARY   *forthcoming

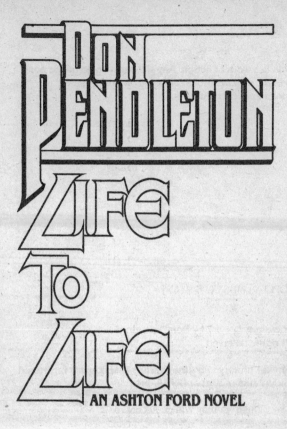

DON PENDLETON

LIFE TO LIFE

AN ASHTON FORD NOVEL

POPULAR LIBRARY

An Imprint of Warner Books, Inc.

A Warner Communications Company

This is a work of fiction. Any similarity to actual persons,
groups, organizations, or events is not intended
and is entirely coincidental.

—dp

POPULAR LIBRARY EDITION

Popular Library® and the fanciful P design are registered
trademarks of Warner Books, Inc.

Cover illustration by Franco Acconero

Popular Library books are published by
Warner Books, Inc.
666 Fifth Avenue
New York, N.Y. 10103

A Warner Communications Company

Printed in the United States of America

First Printing: July, 1987

10 9 8 7 6 5 4 3 2 1

Dedicated to my Muses,
whose names shall not be mentioned here;
and to all the blithe spirits
who read and respond.

dp

AUTHOR'S NOTE

To My Readers:

Ashton Ford will come as something of a surprise to those of you who have been with me over the years. This is not the same type of fiction that established my success as a novelist; Ford is not a gutbuster and he is not trying to save the world from anything but its own confusion. There are no grenade launchers or rockets to solve his problems and he is more of a lover than a fighter.

Some have wondered why I was silent for so many years; some will now also wonder why I have returned in such altered form. The truth is that I had said all I had to say about that other aspect of life. I have grown, I hope, both as a person and as a writer, and I needed another vehicle to carry the creative quest. Ashton Ford is that vehicle. Through this character I attempt to understand more fully and to give better meaning to my perceptions of what is going on here on Planet Earth, and the greatest mystery of all the mysteries: the *why* of existence itself.

Through Ford I use everything I can reach in the total knowledge of mankind to elaborate this mystery and to arm my characters for the quest. I try to entertain myself with their adventures, hoping that what entertains me may also entertain others—so these books, like life itself, are not all grim purpose and trembling truths. They are fun to write; for some they will be fun to read. To each of those I dedicate the work, and I solicit their response. Please let me hear from you, care of Warner Books, 666 Fifth Avenue, New York, NY 10103. My warm best wishes to you all,

Don Pendleton

I hold that when a person dies
His soul returns again to earth;
Arrayed in some new flesh-disguise,
Another mother gives him birth.
With sturdier limbs and brighter brain
The old soul takes the road again.

Such is my own belief and trust;
This hand, this hand that holds the pen,
Has many a hundred times been dust
And turned, as dust, to dust again;
These eyes of mine have blinked and shone
In Thebes, in Troy, in Babylon. . . .

—John Masefield (from *A Creed*)

CHAPTER ONE

Headlong

"Blood!" she cried. "I see blood all over your face!"

I reacted as any normal person would. I raised both hands to my face to check that out. Felt okay to me. Before I could respond verbally, though, Reverend Annie moved on to another seeker of the light and told him, "You will buy the house but you shall never live in it. I see much sorrow there. Sell it quickly. Quickly!"

The guy blinked at her and self-consciously muttered, "Okay. Thank you."

But this gal did not hang around waiting for responses. She'd already gone on to a tense youth of about twenty who was seated several rows back and was approaching him with both hands extended. She wrestled his face into her ample bosom and held him like a mother soothing a beloved child while quietly admonishing him for the "darkness" in his "aura" and calling down "blessings of the light" to assist him "in this dark hour of decision."

It was convincing enough. Not what I would call a "wow show" but the dynamism alone was worth an eight on a scale of ten. She was pretty, she was direct, and she seemed entirely sincere. Of course, they all seem sincere. But Reverend Annie had some subtle essence beyond sincerity that made her something special—which was why I was there.

She'd appeared from obscurity less than a year earlier, rented a storefront in a small shopping center and proclaimed the existence of The Church of the Light. Now she had the entire shopping center and was looking for larger quarters, was conducting fifteen "services" weekly, did a daily radio show, and was gaining prominence in the Hollywood community as the latest trendy advisor to the stars. Thirty-ish and glamorously beautiful when she wanted to be, she was a natural for that scene and seemed to have a good long run ahead of her.

So I'd come out to Van Nuys just to check her out. No fee. Just curiosity. I'd seen them coming and going, these New-Age reverends—only the best came and stayed. Not necessarily the best by virtue of sincerity and validity but the best by virtue of showmanship and charisma. About ninety percent were flatly on the con. The other ten percent were more or less equally divided into those with a genuine interest in helping the human situation but no wherewithal to do so and those with plenty of wherewithal but no interest in anything beyond themselves.

Not that I am a cynic or that I feel particularly qualified to judge these or any other people. To each his own has always been my motto, and that goes double for anything involving religion. It's just that I do have a certain sensitivity for such things and I tend to trust that sensitivity when it tells me I am being conned.

I had not felt conned by Reverend Annie. Even though the "love offering" at the door was twenty bucks and even though her sermon amounted to a mere five minutes of mix-and-match aphorisms from a dozen other religions. There was nothing harmful or hurtful there. There was nothing sinister about the two-minute meditation that followed the sermon, even though it seemed more a plea for money and generosity than anything else. And I was certainly entertained when she swept into the audience and began laying on the hands in her one-on-one ministry even if she did see blood all over my face. You had to be affected also by her looks, be you male or female. Even in vestments she was a wow.

She was a genuine psychic. I had to give her that. She was simply going with the flow, letting it happen, moving from person to person and speaking in total spontaneity. There was no other way to do what she was doing. But I can do that too. Many people can do that, if they'd just let it flow. You have to trust the flow, try not to audit, just run with it—sometimes some amazing shit plops out. Maybe half of what you get is pure static; you give it utterance anyway and just go on. If you hit only one out of four that's enough to build a pile of credibility when people begin comparing notes. Add to that one in four the other ones in four who want so hard to believe that they unconsciously manufacture a hit—and, well, yeah, a one-in-four psychic can quickly become the talk of the town.

I figured that was the case for Annie. The blood on my face sounded like static. How much of the other stuff were direct hits . . . well, I purposely mentioned the two that could be validated on the spot, and they were both right on.

The guy with the house of sorrow was seated at my elbow. He seemed a bit dazed by the experience, told me that indeed he had made an offer on a house in Tarzana that very day. He had mixed feelings about the deal himself, but his wife was crazy about the house so he crossed his fingers and made the offer. Now he didn't know what the hell to do.

The kid with the darkened aura checked out the hardest way. At the conclusion of the service, Reverend Annie had gone to the door to personally greet everyone as they departed. These were small interpersonal gatherings of about fifty people per service—the only way Annie would work but she did it, remember, fifteen times each week. It was a slow dispersal because it seemed that everyone wanted a personal consultation with the beloved Annie. I wanted one too but it had nothing to do with the phantasmal blood on my face. And I wanted more than a minute of her time. So I'd taken a position beside her, and I guess I'd shaken as many hands as she had when the darkened aura began his charge through the patient lineup.

I did not see the gun, not right away, but I did see the dark intent and my reaction was pure instinct. I shoved Annie through the open doorway and threw a crack-back block on the kid in the same movement. We went to the floor together and then I saw the gun. It was a big ugly .357 Magnum and the kid had the barrel in his teeth when we hit the floor. I was close enough to kiss him when he pulled the trigger, close enough to ring my bell when the thing exploded.

Of course I thought I was shot. I was lying stunned in the gore with hysteria breaking out all around me. Then Reverend Annie had me by each hand, tugging me away from that, coolly coaxing me to my feet, guiding me toward a chair. I caught my reflection in a window. And, yeah, there was blood all over my face. So. What the hell. Three out of three ain't bad.

The dead man turns out to be one Herman Milhaul. Has a long history of mental instability, though he is only now twenty. Seems that he is homosexual, has been trying to have a sex-change operation. Terribly unhappy young man. Reverend Annie has seen him before. He has attended several of her services over the past couple of weeks but has never sought her personal counsel. She believes that he came to this particular service to kill both her and himself, though she has no explanation for that.

The cops are taking their time on this one. There were still about twenty persons present at the time of the incident. We have all been removed to a classroom next door and each of us has been interviewed more than once. Reverend Annie patiently tells the same story over and over, each time crediting me with saving her life.

The L.A. cops are very good, very efficient. Van Nuys is one of those satellite communities that comprise the bulk of L.A.'s population, geographically delineated within the San Fernando Valley but politically just another L.A. neighborhood. Much of what is generally referred to as the Hollywood community actually live in the valley; many of them work here, as well. Be advised that "the community" refers to more than actors. They are just the tip of the largely unseen iceberg that keeps those actors in public view.

So it is no great surprise to also learn that Herman Milhaul is one of these, that he has worked for the past year as a film lab technician. Actually, more than half the witnesses to his dramatic suicide are members of the industry. Two are even recognizable as character actors on television. Reverend Annie, as I have noted, is big with the business, as they say. I am a bit surprised to discover (by eavesdropping), however, that one of the witnesses—a handsome man of about seventy—is one of the most respected and honored screenwriters. Writers are, I always thought, intellectual people, and intellectual people, by and large, do not buy the Reverend Annies of the world. Or so I think. I am to be proven wrong on that. I am, in fact, to be proven wrong on many misconceptions before this case is ended.

At the moment though, I do not know there is a case. I have come to watch a much-heralded psychic at work, I have been entertained by what I saw, and then I have found myself involved in the self-inflicted death of a tormented young man who saw only darkness in his life so had opted for a better berth elsewhere. The ultimate sex change, maybe. Or maybe...

But this is about where I am in my head when the cops turn us loose. I have been cleaned up a bit, but my clothes are a mess and dried flecks of blood are in my hair. Reverend Annie pulls me aside and embraces me. "You saved my life," she murmurs. "I saw it coming. I saw it. He intended to take me with him."

"When did you first see it coming?" I ask.

"During one-on-one. I knew he'd come to kill me."

"So why didn't you just get out of here? Why—?"

"Because I saw something else, too," she coolly informs me. "I saw you. Each time, we learn to accept; to trust. I knew that you would save me. As for poor Herman... Nothing could save him. We learn to accept that, too."

She releases me, steps back—teary-eyed—starts to walk

away, stops, looks back, says: "We shall meet again. We shall fall in love."

I send her a smile. I am a bit of a psychic too, you know. "Scary, isn't it," is my response to Reverend Annie.

She shivers, gives me a solemn little smile, then walks away.

And I am now heading into the most interesting case I have ever encountered. It will send me backward into the golden age of Hollywood and maybe into the outskirts of another golden age that Hollywood never dreamt of—and it will send me very close to hell itself.

But, of course, hell itself is precisely where it started.

CHAPTER
TWO

And a Cymbal Clashed...

David Carver, a homicide detective, was waiting for me beside my Maserati. I knew him slightly. Know a lot of cops, but mostly just enough to smile and say "Hi" if we pass on the street. Carver was in that class. Cops don't make the best of friends, except with other cops. They lead mean lives. Sort of takes one to appreciate one. There are exceptions, of course. Not many. Doesn't mean I don't respect cops. Mostly I do. Carver I did.

He grinned and said, "Hi, Ash. Saw your name on the sheets."

I told him, "I gave my statement to Lieutenant Stewart."

He said, "Yeah, I know. Read it. Just want to talk to you. Off the record. Okay?"

I said, "David . . . look at me . . . I need a hot shower and a change of clothes. Make it quick?"

"Sure. What's with you and the reverend?"

I shrugged. "I was just a face in the crowd."

"You weren't bodyguarding her?"

I gave him what I hoped was a disgusted look. "Things are not that bad, David. I do not guard bodies other than those that are in my bed."

"Wasn't your gun, eh?"

I showed him another attempt at disgust. "When I pull a trigger, pal, I want the machine to gently purr, not bust my hand apart." I showed him the hand in question. "Designed especially to hold a tennis racquet, not a snorting .357 Magnum. All my arms are registered. Check it out."

"Already did," he said, still grinning genially. "Where's your Walther?"

I inclined my head toward the car and replied, "Inside."

"Show me."

I sighed, unlocked the car, removed the pistol from its concealed floorboard compartment, handed it over to him. He smiled and handed it back, told me: "You'd better start carrying it."

I knew better than to ask but did so anyway. "Why?"

"I mean if you plan on keeping company with the reverend."

"I didn't say I planned on that. We haven't even been formally introduced."

"That's good," he said. "Keep it that way."

So I asked it again. "Why?"

"This kid Milhaul is the third violent death in her congregation over the past two months. One more makes an epidemic. Sounds like you damn near qualified for that one tonight. A word to the wise, Ash."

I told him, "Hell, I just came down to look her over. And I—"

"What'd you see?"

I gave the homicide detective a steady gaze as I replied, "I saw a screwed-up kid try to kill her. I intervened in that. Call it bodyguarding if you like but it was pure coincidence that it was me instead of someone else."

"Sure of that?" he asked, the grin still in place.

I said, "What is this, Carver? You didn't just happen to . . ."

He replied, "Naw. The lieutenant thought it would be best if I talked to you out here. Privately, you know." He handed over a slip of paper. I unfolded it, stared at it for a couple of seconds, handed it back.

Two names were written on that paper in a curiously stilted scrawl. Mine and the dead boy's. They were enclosed in brackets.

I asked, "So where'd you find it?"

He replied, "In the reverend's study, small room just behind the stage. Says she always meditates back there before each service."

"Is that her handwriting?"

"Not her normal handwriting, no. But she claims it. Calls it her guide's hand."

"Her guide's hand," I muttered.

"Yeah. Like automatic writing. Trance stuff."

I said, "Yeah."

"She says she wrote that before the service."

I said, "Yeah."

"Is that nutty, or what?"

I shrugged. "Yeah."

"Which one?"

"Both," I said.

He asked, "Do you know the lady or don't you?"

I told him, "I saw her for the first time at eight o'clock tonight. I was in the audience. She was on the stage. She talked. I listened. Far as I know, she'd never heard my name until I gave it to the officer an hour or so later. Since then we have spoken. For about thirty seconds. Just before I stepped out here. Do I *know* the lady? Hell no. But you can bet your ass, pal, that I am *going* to know the lady."

"Want to work with us?"

I looked him up and down. "Fee?"

He looked me up and down. "Expenses, maybe."

I said, "I'll let you know."

He said, "You're involved, Ash, whether you know it or not. Either someone set you up, or—"

I said, "That's nutty. I came over here on an impulse. Happened to be in the general area, decided to check her out. Nobody knew I was coming. Didn't know it myself even until the very last minute. I am not involved, David."

He waggled the note paper under my nose and said, "Bullshit."

I said, "Expenses?"

He said, "Yeah, I'm sure I can do that much for you."

I told him, "Call you tomorrow. Right now . . ."

He stepped back, said, "Yeah. You look terrible. Smell even worse. The reverend should have taken you to the showers."

I got in the car, cranked it, said to him through the open window, "She's not married, eh?"

"Not lately. Pretty good track record, though."

"How good is pretty good?"

"Four times a widow. I call it a perfect record."

I grunted, set the Maserati in motion, made tracks for the Ventura Freeway. I live at Malibu. That is not exactly next door to Van Nuys. I figured I had close to an hour's drive ahead of me. And Carver was right. I smelled bad. Herman Milhaul was clinging to me. I really wanted to wash him away. So I drove like a maniac. I made it home in thirty minutes flat.

More than the splattered remains of Herman Milhaul was driving me that way. I had the feeling, and the feeling wasn't good. Something was coming down my pike. And I . . .

Oh. Maybe you don't know yet. I'm Ashton Ford. I'm sort of psychic. I'm also sort of a detective but . . . no, that doesn't really wash, I am not a detective by any stretch of the imagination. But I have developed a sort of a reputation as . . . some people call me the mystic eye—but I really do not think I am a mystic and I do not carry a badge of any kind so . . . I play tennis. Not professionally, not that good. Even if I was, I wouldn't do it for a living. That would take all the fun out of it. Guess I don't do anything for a living . . . probably for the same reason. But I'm fortunate. My mother was one of the South Carolina Ashtons. That means I was born with a trust fund. Nothing spectacular, but it buys the groceries and pays the rent, gives me a certain freedom. So I do pretty much what I want to do with my time. I am aware of the privilege. Not apologetic, but aware. So I try to give something back, now and then.

I have done some work for the police. Missing persons mostly, but I have been in on some homicides too. I usually do it for free unless one of the bureaus has a little extra in the budget.

I also do private consulting. Don't ask what that means. I don't know what that means. But it sounds nice, for what I do.

At that moment, arriving home with Herman's decaying hemoglobin clinging to my clothing, I wanted to do nothing but shower and go to bed.

But I had a visitor. He had been waiting for me, he said, for quite some time. He introduced himself as Bruce Janulski, and told me that he was Ann Farrel's personal secretary. Ann Farrel is Reverend Annie. Bruce is a beautiful, golden giant—about six-four, broad of shoulder and narrow in the flanks—a genuine goddam Adonis, but Bruce, I gather after about ten seconds, would be little more than a frustration to any of the opposite sex. This guy is a *gentle-* man. He does not walk, he sways; he does not talk, he sings; and his palms are forever turned heavenward.

I was not asking this guy in for a drink—though I wanted a drink probably even more strongly than I wanted a shower. We talked in the carport. I asked him, "How'd you get here so quick?"

He gave me a perplexed look as he replied, "But I have been here for an *hour,* Mr. Ford."

I told him, a bit brusquely, "That's not possible. I left Annie's just a half an hour ago myself."

He said, "Oh *damn* it"—quietly but sort of pouting. "I came all the way out here for *nothing* then. I mean, if you've been *together* . . ."

I said, "Now wait a minute . . ."

He pulled his Member's Only jacket closer about the muscled chest and shivered. "Why didn't someone *tell* me it gets this cold at the ocean? I am freezing to *death.*"

I relented then and asked the poor guy in. After all . . .

He said, "No, no, thank you, I'll just scoot on back."

I asked, "What time did she send you, Bruce?"

His eyes crackled with confidentiality as he replied, "Well, *she* did not send me, Mr. Ford. I came on my own."

I was getting tired of this word: "Why?"

"Well, because I feel that she is in great danger."

"You should go to the police."

"Not that kind of danger."

"What kind, then?"

"Your kind, Mr. Ford."

"How do you know what kind I am?"

"Heavens, I'd never heard of you until just a few hours ago. I consulted my guides. *They* sent me to you."

"Your guides."

"Yes. But it appears that they reached you directly. Thank goodness. Did you have a nice visit?"

I said, "Look at me, Bruce. Do I look like a guy coming home from a nice visit anywhere?"

He seemed to notice my appearance for the first time. He recoiled; gasped, "Good heavens! What has happened?"

"Trouble—the police kind—has happened," I told him. "Herman Milhaul tried to kill your Annie. Don't worry, he failed, but I think you'd better get back there right away."

"Who in the world is Herman Milhaul?" he squeaked.

"Nobody, now, in this world," I told him. "Go home." But he did not hear that, did not need to hear it. Bruce was already on his way home. He leaped into his car and tore out of there under about three G's.

I went on into the house, stripped totally naked just inside the door, paused at the bar for bourbon and water, and took it with me to the shower. The phone started ringing before I got the water adjusted to the right temperature. I have an answer for Murphy's telephone law; I keep a phone in the bathroom.

But I wished I'd let it ring.

It was François Mirabel. Yeah, *that* François Mirabel, producer to the stars. And he wanted me to hop right back to town and defend Reverend Annie's life with my very own.

Well, what the hell. Between the cops, spirit guides, and the one and only François—not to mention the pretty reverend herself—how does a tennis bum like me say no?

No matter—I had already said yes; the rest was mere timing. Or had the timing already begun even before I'd heard the question? Probably, yeah. I live in that kind of world, see. The end is reached before the beginning begins and both exist in the here and now. Time and space are mere constructs of the human mind, relativity is an abstract, one is all and all are one, existence itself is a single clash of the cymbal. In that world, nothing is for sure and everything is possible.

Even a Reverend Annie is possible.

Never mind all the others. I intended to find out for myself.

C H A P T E R
T H R E E

In the Aura

François maintains a swank palace in Beverly Hills but he is not there a lot, dividing his time mostly between a couple of other places he owns in Europe. He has also not bothered to cultivate spoken English beyond the marginally intelligible level. I speak French not at all. We have a language problem. We have known each other for several years but very casually, which is the way I prefer it. François thinks the world is his very own playpen.

It was well past midnight when I reached his place, but it was bristling with light from every window and the drive was filled with cars. I had to park on the street. I do not like to leave the Maserati on any street anywhere at any time so I went in with a small chip already in place upon the shoulder.

A party, as usual, was in progress. I detest name-dropping

so I won't do that. Just be aware that this gathering would be enough to induce terminal orgasmic tremors in your average autograph hound. Some fifty to sixty people, I'd guess; the hot ones of screen and television mixed here and there with writers and directors. This is the way François conducted business, negotiated deals, packaged productions. He threw a party, invited possible candidates, mixed and matched them until something fell out. Although his name is emblazoned across screens anywhere, François does not actually produce pictures, or write them, or direct them. He does not read scripts—does not even view his own movies, I am told. Likes to think of himself as a catalyst. Actually he is a financier and, of course, he owns what falls out.

Listening to him describe the process—in his limited use of the language—is like hearing one of those high school cheerleaders: "Give me an M—give me an O—give me an N . . ."

François would say, "Give me persons and I rearrange them to spell 'money.' Give me director. Give me writer. Give me leading man, leading lady. Do not give me picture. *They* will give me picture and *it* will give me money."

He was in it for the money. An honest man. Or was he? I sometimes wondered if François simply loved the party and was not afraid to invest in it. He also, I had observed, trusted his instincts—which is another way of saying that he played hunches.

I found him holding court on a sofa in the very eye of the party. Reverend Annie was seated beside him. She wore a stunning toga-style white gown, one shoulder bared, the dark hair swept over that shoulder in a most appealing way. François sprang to his feet at my approach and gave me a warm embrace, slapping my back and beaming and saying,

"Good boy," over and over. Annie was watching my discomfort with a veiled gaze while François announced my heroism to the party at large, even led them in a round of applause. Then he excused us and dragged me off to the library for a private conference.

This guy is about sixty I think—who would know? Still dynamic and handsome—very youthful, actually—dancing eyes and bubbling enthusiasm, but not overdone. I mean, you know, not tiresome. He could get mean as hell, too. He could also switch from a twinkle in the eye to a shrewd business gleam in a single blink so you never knew precisely where you stood from moment to moment.

He threw one of those at me the moment we were alone, nailing me with a no-nonsense glare as he inquired, "What is happen?"

I shrugged and reminded him, "You just told the folks what is happen, François."

"I told what?"

"Never mind," I said. "You already have it. It happened like you said. That's all I know about it."

"Speak straight to me, Ashton."

I lit a cigarette, went to the desk and sat on it, told him while gazing at the floor, "Straight as I can find it, pal. I'd heard of Annie. Who hasn't in this town by now? Never met her, though. Went to check her out tonight. Purely an impulse. I was in the neighborhood. The time was right. I had nothing better to do. So I checked her out. As I was leaving, this guy made a lunge at her. I intervened. He died. She didn't. Some hero. A twenty-year-old disturbed human being died tonight, François."

I wasn't sure how much of that he was getting but he commented at that point, "Better he than she."

-18-

I shrugged and said, "Maybe. Point is, I don't feel like a hero. So let's leave off with the applause, eh?"

"They love her!" he cried, coming at me with one hand held high overhead and the other leading the way toward me, almost in a fencing posture. "All love her! Soon the whole world will love her! And *I*, Ashton, have a piece of that!"

I said, quietly, "Congratulations."

"Sure, congratulations!" He sat down beside me atop the desk and swung his feet in idle circles.

I asked, "Going to make her a movie star?"

"Nah. Small stuff. Have you regarded the religion business lately, Ashton?"

I said, "That what it is?"

"What else? It is commerce. Commerce is money. Ipso-ipso, religion is money."

I said, "That's pretty cynical, isn't it?"

"Ask the Pope. Ask the Vatican Bank."

"Come on."

He grinned. "Ask your television evangelists."

"That what you have in mind for her?"

"It is her mind, Ashton," he said with a hurt tone. "You know I do not create. I underwrite."

I suggested, "You'd better look into U.S. law and the internal revenue code before you underwrite this one, pal. Could get your tit in a real wringer on something like this."

"What does this mean? Tits do not ring."

I said, "Yours will if you start playing producer to the reverends. Anyway..."

"Anyway," he said after a moment, "you must continue in this."

"This what?"

"These attempts on her life. You must prevent."

I said, "François, I—"

He headed me off with: "Name your price."

I said, "That is not the issue. I had already decided, even before you called, that I—"

"It is by her request, Ashton."

"What do you mean?"

"She has request your protection."

"Annie asked . . . ?"

"Yes."

I said, "Well, I'd already decided . . . okay. You're going to underwrite the thing?"

"But of course. She is hot property. Do not allow her to grow cold."

"Level with me, François," I requested. "Annie is more than another hot property to you. Right?"

He twinkled at me. "Right. So take very good care in my behalf."

I said okay and we returned to the party.

Annie was entertaining a small group gathered at the sofa. As we walked up she was telling an aging female star who shall remain nameless: "Yes, this is very positive, you will be working again before the end of this year. I don't get his name but a really big writer is at this moment doing the final polish on a beautiful screenplay designed specifically with you in mind as the female lead. I should think that you will be seeing this script within just a few days. Go with it. It's right for you."

The actress was beaming at this news. She asked, "Can I hold you to that?"

"Positively," Annie replied. "Write it down if you'd like and date it. I'll sign it."

There was an impressed murmur from the group. The actress wanted more detail. "What sort of role? Do you see...?"

Which is the point at which good old Ashton blundered in. It was pure faux pas and I don't know to this day why I did it. I am really not a show-off and I am usually respectful of other people's turf. But I was standing in Annie's limelight without even realizing it, and my jaw was moving without the thinking mind telling it to do so. It was almost like absentminded, like replying to a question while your head is buried in a book.

"It's a story about a nun who becomes a prostitute in Paris during the Nazi occupation to save the fleeing Jews."

Yep. Ashton said that. Annie's eyes were giving me a measuring look.

I recovered, I think, to the satisfaction of everyone except Annie. "Kidding," I said with a chuckle. "Sorry, folks. I have to take the reverend away from you." I took her hand and pulled her out of there. François followed us. As soon as we were clear I told Annie, "Sorry 'bout that. Just sort of slipped out. Like gas. Please accept my apology. More importantly, I want you to know that I want to work this problem with you and I think we need to start a game plan."

The lady was showing me a very haughty look. The gaze swept to François then back to me as she said, "I'm sorry, Mr. Ford. I do not see anything positive here."

"Not blood on my face again, surely," I said, still trying to keep it light.

"I see death in your aura."

I said, "Then maybe we better work up a game plan for me."

"What is—?" François ventured only to be shut down by the frigid reverend.

"That would be quite impossible, I'm afraid," she said icily. "Good night, Mr. Ford."

I looked at François and François looked at me.

I said to Annie, "Good night to you too," and went the hell away from there.

Death in my aura, huh?

Shit. There is death in every aura.

And the good Reverend Annie was a lady with a lot to hide.

CHAPTER
FOUR

Waiting in the Stream

Let's get it into the record, right up front here, that I am not antireligion. Many of mankind's noblest moments have come in the religious quest—our most exalted art, music, literature, even architecture—the whole search for identity as a living species has been largely propelled not by the practical requirements for survival but by an aesthetic appreciation of the divine possibilities within us.

It would almost seem that the innate human penchant for religiosity represents the spiritual equivalent of physical evolution. How else could we dare reach for the stars—and why otherwise develop the technologies that could put us there?

So I do not knock religion per se. My respect for the edifice does not, however, prevent me from noticing the chipped bricks, broken windows, or sagging foundations that appear from time to time. Churches contain toilets as well as pews, so not everything going down within the edifice is necessarily sacred—unless there is some basis for the expression *holy shit*.

Devoutly religious people sometimes do irreligious things. The same is true of entire religious bodies, unless you'd rather just forget about the horrors of the Inquisition, the burning of "witches" in New England, the acceptance of human slavery in young America, etc. *ad nauseam*. None of that, however, invalidates for me the religious instinct.

Where we go wrong, I think—so many of us, and so often—is in our resistance to fair and impartial inquiry. Either we defend the faith so stoutly that we refuse (or are afraid) to look at the broken windows, or else we are so cynical that we will see nothing else.

François Mirabel's remarks about the religion industry were rather typical of that latter point of view. Yet the religionists themselves promote that sort of cynicism through their dogged insistence upon the infallibility of their own limited view.

There are scoundrels in religion. Why not admit that, expose them when we discover them, and go on with the quest?

There are errors in religion. Why not admit it, correct them when we find them, and go on with the quest?

But see, the problem—the real problem—is that none of us are gods or angels yet. We are human. Therefore we all possess to some degree every aspect of the human inheritance. And that estate includes arrogance as well as humility, greed as well as charity, fear as well as love, and all the other opposites of human personality. A good man can be moved to do an evil thing; an evil man can be moved to do a good thing.

François said that religion is money. That is true. But it is also good works, inspired acts, noble aspirations, and blind faith that man is more than a common animal.

With that in the record, let's go on now to consider this "religion industry." How big is it? It's *big*. The annual take of the combined churches of North America alone greatly exceeds the national income of most of the world's nations. In the United States, this runs close to thirty *billion* dollars every year. That figure does not include the haul of radio and television preachers or any of the itinerant evangelists, storefront groups or street-corner prophets. It does not include the activities of organizations such as the Hare Krishnas, the ashrams, the horde of gurus like Maharaj Ji and Rajneesh, outfits like Scientology, or any of the New Age groups. No one I have run across would venture a guess as to how much money accrues to these others. I will so venture, and I'd put it as roughly equal to that of the traditional churches. So we could be talking sixty billion dollars a year in this country alone. That is a lot of bread cast upon the waters of man's faith in something larger than himself.

So much bread, in fact, that it sometimes creates a feeding frenzy among those waiting in the stream.

Is religion money? Of course it is. And money is like blood in the stream of life, crazing the sharks who patrol the eddies of the stream.

Is François a shark? Of course he is.

So what is Reverend Annie? Only time—and enough blood—would tell.

* * *

"She's thirty-five years old, born in Azusa, graduated from Hollywood High seventeen years ago, married a classmate two weeks later, left him two weeks after that; he died by suicide while her petition for annulment was pending; let's see . . . worked in a fast-food restaurant, later as a cocktail waitress, married again at twenty-one; this one died of a heart attack in the third year . . . ummm . . . a gap here of several years . . . pick her up again at twenty-eight with her third marriage; that one died in a fiery freeway crash almost exactly a year later . . . identification by dental charts . . . she's at Pomona Valley College, psychology; short try at nursing school, Mount Sac; then to UCLA, more psychology, no degree . . . another short run at Science of Mind Institute, did not complete . . . ummm . . . okay, here it is, married the last victim four years ago, and she's in her present name now; guy was a cinematographer, guess he did okay before he married her; uh, slipped in the bathtub, says here . . . died without regaining consciousness . . . three months in coma . . . declared brain-dead, and disconnected from life support at spouse's request . . ."

"When was this?"

"Fifteen months ago."

"Uh huh. And she chartered the church—"

"Four months later."

"I see."

Actually I saw nothing whatever. I'd taken a chance on finding David Carver still at work at such an hour, dropped in on him, found him very hard at work and totally immersed in the enigma of Reverend Annie. Seems that he was putting a lot of his own time into this. There was no case on Annie. The cases were . . .

"Maybelle Flossie Turner, age seventy-two, widow, died of asphyxiation, gas leak, in her small apartment on March 14th. Her entire estate, valued at $22,832, went to Church of Light. Ann Farrel is executor."

"Eight weeks ago."

"Right. Then there is Charles Cohan McSweeney, age fifty-seven, reclusive bachelor—committed twice to Camarillo for child molestation, number of pornography indictments but no convictions—shot by police officer while resisting arrest on April 21st on complaint by—who else?—our Annie."

"Five weeks later."

"About that. And then yesterday, of course . . ."

I sighed and asked, "What was the complaint?"

Carver sighed too. "Indecent exposure and child fondling. In the church's nursery."

"For that he died."

"If for anything at all. Then last night the Milhaul kid. We're talking two months here, Ash, and three deaths that should not have been. There is a common denominator here and its name is not coincidence."

I shrugged and suggested, "Don't leap off the deep end too fast, David."

"Bullshit, don't give me that. I haven't found it yet but there's a tie somewhere. My gut knows it's true and the gut will not let go. This woman is like that Al Capp character, the little guy with the dark cloud always above him. Don't forget the four poor souls that married her. And all this is just what's in the *record*. God what I wouldn't give for a crystal ball!"

"You think maybe I've got one, eh?" I muttered.

"If not," he said, "then something just as good. I've seen your work. And let me tell—"

"I don't have one," I said flatly. "But..."

"But what?"

"I'm going to give it a whirl."

He grinned. "Hell, I knew that."

"See?" I said. "Anyone can read minds."

Carver kept on grinning as he inquired, "Where would you like to start?"

I told him, "Well, I'll...need to do some thinking and..." I showed him a smile. "Same as you, pal, the old-fashioned way. I'll have to scrape some shoe leather."

"Scraping for vibes, eh?"

"Something like that, yeah."

"Great. You need any doors opened, just let me know. Otherwise I guess you're on your own. Captain doesn't give me a lot of time for my gut. Right now we got a case load like you wouldn't believe. But I am pulling an early-morning—I tracked down one of Maybelle's old friends, sweet old gal up near Pasadena. Talked to her on the phone just this evening. She's an early riser; likes to spend her mornings feeding the birds in the park. So I've got a date at eight with Clara. She's going to bake up some fresh blue-berry muffins and we're going to breakfast on her patio." He shot me a wink. "She's seventy-five. Want to make it a threesome?"

I winced and said, "Not if that's eight in the morning." Hell, it was already three o'clock; I'd be lucky to get to bed by four. "Let me know how you make out with Clara, though. I have a mobile number so you can..." I handed him a card. "It works most of the time. There's a message number there too if you have trouble running me down."

Carver grinned, said, "Shit, I figured you always *knew* when someone's trying to reach you."

"Female only," I said, and left him at his desk.

I would not be seeing the young detective again, nor would he be trying me at any of my terrestrial numbers.

Clara killed him at eight-thirty that morning.

CHAPTER FIVE

Sweet Memory

I don't mind saying that I am feeling a bit ragged at this point. David Carver and I have not exactly been friends, but he is a cop I have liked and respected so I feel the loss. Also I am experiencing mental fatigue along with something else I can only describe as a sort of spiritual brownout. It is nearly noon and I am seated in the office of Paul Stewart, Carver's boss. The lieutenant is clearly upset and feeling at least as ragged as I. He and Carver were close friends so his sense of loss is stronger than mine. I am aware of a growing anger building close beneath that layer of grief. I do not know which way he is most likely to blow so I am prepared for anything. I am simply keeping my thoughts to myself, quietly going through the case file that Carver had been developing in the Church of Light matter.

Clara Boone sits just outside the cubicle. She seems dazed, unsure of exactly where she is and what is happening here. She has not been charged with any crime. It is likely that Carver's death will be ruled accidental and that no charges of any kind will be filed. Actually Clara is free to leave whenever she herself is ready to do that. Problem is, she is obviously not ready to do that and apparently there is no one at home to help her.

This is the way it happened, the best as Stewart and his people can put it together. Carver kept his eight o'clock appointment; he and Clara ate a light breakfast and talked on her patio. We don't know what they talked about. But Carver was done and ready to leave at eight-thirty. Clara was prepared to leave immediately behind him. She always fed her birds at a nearby park, same time every morning seven days a week rain or shine, and she was running a few minutes late and anxious about that.

Carver said good-bye and went to his vehicle which was parked at the curb in front of her house. He did not leave right away, though; apparently he sat there for several minutes and went over some notes he'd taken during the interview. Clara's car was in her garage. Carver was still on the scene when she backed it onto the narrow drive outside. She was getting out of the car to close the garage door when Carver appeared on foot to help her. He closed the garage door for her. She put the car into reverse, she thought, preparing to back on out to the street. But then her sack of birdseed toppled over and began spilling onto the seat. She made a grab for the birdseed. Next thing she knew Detective Carver was pinned to her garage door by the grill of her car. It is an old car, with a fancy hood ornament up front. The

ornament pierced Carver's heart. He died instantly. This is
the story as it appears on the official report.

Stewart has granted me access to Carver's files. There is
also the small notebook that was found on the seat of his
vehicle opened to some hastily jotted, cryptic notes—apparently covering his visit with Clara. I have made several trips
to the copy machine and I now have duplicates of the more
pertinent items in Carver's file as well as his final notes.

Frankly, I do not have a hell of a lot of anything. The gut
does not translate too well into official reports. Most of what
Carver had working was in the gut. Apparently Lt. Stewart
had not shared his subordinate's suspicions about the web of
coincidence enshrouding Ann Farrel and the rash of violent
deaths; even now his buried anger seems to have no direction and therefore no outlet.

This is where I am; where we are; and poor befuddled
Clara seated just outside the door.

I got to my feet and said, "Thanks, Lieutenant. And, uh,
thanks for the notification."

"What do you have in mind?" he asked gruffly.

I threw up the hands; told him, "The mind is fibrillating
right now. I don't know what the hell. Except that David
really thought he had something here. I told him last night
I'd give it a whirl. So . . . I guess . . ."

"I'll put you on a voucher," Stewart said quietly. "Keep
me advised."

I said, "Sure," and went on out.

Clara showed me a confused smile.

I stopped, turned around, returned to the office, asked
Stewart, "Mind if I take Clara home?"

He gave me a very short look and replied with eyes already withdrawn, "Not at all."

So I gave the lady my arm and we both went away from there. It was intended as a gentle courtesy. Turned out to be the smartest thing I'd done all year.

Clara lives at the northeast fringe of the city in the Eagle Rock area. Couple of blocks east and her house would have been situated in the city of Pasadena. By freeway it's only about twenty minutes from downtown, but Clara had not ventured this far south since shortly after the end of World War II. No wonder she was disoriented. L.A. has changed a lot over the years. Whole new high-rise skyline. The fantastic freeway interchanges with their tiers of ramps curving away in every direction, literally highways in the sky. The downtown traffic in all its frenzy, packs of trucks and busses all running with too much abandon and not nearly enough courtesy toward the old, the timid, and the confused.

Clara had never even seen Dodger Stadium. I tried to point it out to her as we buzzed past Chavez Ravine, but we were moving too fast in too much company and I doubt that she was particularly interested anyway. Guess she thought I was a cop. She did not understand why her car had been impounded, and I could tell by the look in her eyes that she was wondering how she would ever get it back to Eagle Rock. We did not talk a lot during that drive except for comments on the traffic and the passing scenery. I knew that her mind was still clouded and I did not want to add to that. So we small-talked, when at all, and I simply left her to find her own mind her own way.

I think the drive settled her down a bit. She perked up noticeably when we reached familiar territory and she was checking her hair in the visor mirror when I pulled into her driveway. It was one of the old-style California bungalows, small stucco with a red-tile roof, maybe as old as her but

neat and trim and probably very gracious inside. I wondered
idly what the years had brought to her through that home—
how much joy?—how many regrets? Was the sum total of
Clara Boone contained within those stucco walls?

Maybe she was wondering the same thing at the same
time. If so, it had not been all joy because she was gazing at
that house with obvious distaste. Or maybe it was just the
immediate past that was on her mind. She asked me, "Is the
young man going to be all right?"

Damn! She didn't even realize that . . .

I told her, "It's okay, Clara."

"This was a very nice neighborhood at one time," she said
wistfully.

I could believe that. But all things change. I asked her,
very gently, "Is there someone you could stay with for a few
days?"

"No one," she replied without even wondering about it.

A car had pulled up across the street. A guy was fussing
with camera equipment. The insatiable press had smelt the
blood.

I thought about it for all of two seconds then asked Clara,
"Would you like to spend a few days at the beach?"

"Oh I couldn't afford that," she said with a small laugh.

"My guest," I told her. "I have a place at Malibu."

"Really! At the colony?"

The small laugh was mine this time. She was talking me-
gabucks there. I replied, "No, but on a really clear day I can
see their roofs. What do you say? There's a spare bedroom
and I promise to behave myself."

Those old eyes had begun to sparkle. "I spent a weekend
at the colony once."

My turn. "Really!"

"Yes. But that was a very long time ago. I haven't been to the ocean since . . ."

I said, "Then you're overdue." The guy with the cameras was out of his vehicle now, gazing our way. "Why don't you run in and put a few things together?"

"You know, I think I will!"

"Good girl. Scoot. I'll wait for you here."

She was moving like a twenty-year-old as she crossed to the house, and the look she tossed me over the shoulder as she went inside was, I swear, almost vampish. The reporter hurried over and was making his way along the walk when I stepped out of the car. He ignored me, went on to the door, and was about to push the bell when I warned him, "Ring that bell, pal, and I'll ring yours."

He swiveled about to give me a respectful look, finger still poised at the doorbell, and said the magic word. "Press."

I said mine. "Uh-uh."

He was flustered and appropriately outraged but also a man of reason. "I'd like to at least get some pictures of the scene," he muttered.

I said, "Take all you'd like after we're gone. That will be just a minute or so. Meanwhile, vacate the property. Please."

The reporter took the "please" in the spirit it was given, immediately retreating to his vehicle.

I leaned against the Maserati and lit a cigarette, scowling his way occasionally until Clara reappeared in the doorway with a small overnight bag in her hand. I went over and took it from her, put them both in the car, and we took off for Malibu.

"This is terrible," she told me with a giggle. "I don't even remember your name."

I arched my eyebrows at her and told her back, sounding almost like François, "Never fear, *ma cherie*, it shall be on your lips the whole night through."

She loved it.

Hell, so did I.

A minute or so later Clara gave me a very direct but almost embarrassed look then smiled soberly and asked me, "Don't you have the feeling that we've done this before?"

Yes. I did. I had that feeling very strongly.

CHAPTER
SIX

In an Envelope of Time

Ever consider how important *memory* is to the living organism? Any living organism. Birds have it. Bees have it. Bugs in the tree have it. The tree itself has it. Otherwise there would be no two living things that were really similar. Life is a dynamic force. It gathers up diffusing matter and molds it into an image of itself. Without the mold there would be only the gathering and it could be as diffuse as hydrogen gas or as dense as a black hole in space. Which is to say, without life.

The black hole and the hydrogen are formed by other processes, but even these require a more elemental kind of memory and they definitely are the result of molds in space.

In elemental life forms, this *memory* for expression is carried within microscopic bits of fluff which man in his genius has labeled *genes*. To *call* a bowl of peanuts a bowl of beans does not change the taste of the peanuts. Man's penchant for naming things (since Adam) gets us all into a lot of trouble because we do not all of us call the same things by the same names.

We do love to package things too, and of course the practice has proven highly convenient—so when I ask for a hot dog most people know that what I want is a wiener on a bun with maybe a slap of mustard. Ask an aborigine for a hot dog, though, and he's liable to set fire to your French poodle.

So the word *gene* is just a handy way of packaging a very esoteric idea long before we got around to understanding the idea itself. Early biologists recognized the fact that all living things carry a set of instructions locked up inside them and that these instructions are sort of like blueprints by which that living thing was constructed—and it was noted that these instructions are the means by which hereditary characteristics are transmitted from parent to offspring. So what the hell, let's call these instructions *genes*, from the Greek *genea* which means breed or kind. We could just as easily have called them *mems* and been much closer to the truth.

If life is a dynamic force that collects inert matter and molds it into an image of itself, and if a certain *kind* of life always works from the same mold generation after generation to construct an edifice of expression which only it may inhabit, then those *molds* can only be the *memories* of past successful expressions or incarnations because no other definition makes any sense at all.

Take a note. Write this down. Better sketch that. Make a map. Record it.

Jottings. Genes are jottings, cryptic notes, recipes for successful forays into the space-time dimension. It is a kind of memory. And a book of memories, pal, is more or less what you and I really are. Of course we have the advantage over slugs and snails because we are a much more complex organism and so our book is much thicker and probably carries a lot more footnotes. We are so complex indeed that our memory-pak includes a kit for great masses of nerve tissue put together in a very special way that allows the development of a whole new kind of memory—and this nerve-tissue memory in turn produces something called *personality* or, as my dictionary defines the term, "that which constitutes a person; personal existence."

So you and I have genetic memory and personal memory. The genetic memory has much to say about how tall you are, the color of your hair and eyes, susceptibility to certain diseases, special affinities and talents, and it even has something to say about the way you handle personal memory.

Personal memory becomes a way that we regard ourselves, our relation to nature and to one another. We are really talking about *experience* now but the experience has to be remembered if it is to have an effect upon our personalities. Indeed it is the memory of the experience more so than the experience itself that builds personality so we are still talking about memory. If you show the kid every morning how to tie his shoes but you are still tying them for him when he's in high school, then the experience has helped him not a bit. Only when he remembers does the experience take on meaning.

The important thing to remember there is that you never had to show the kid how to circulate blood through his body.

His little heart began beating quite ahead of any direct influence from you because he remembered genetically how to start it up and keep it regulated, the same as he remembered how to build it and the blood too along with everything else he brought here with him.

The genetic memory establishes *species* and space-time orientation. In other words, a man and a woman cannot pool their mems to provide a space-time envelope for a pig memory. Only pigs can do that. But the pig memory cannot work with the highly complex construction kit for humans—only human memory can do that—so pigs will never tie shoes, no matter how many times you show them how.

Nerve memory produces unique personalities within a species. The more complex the kit, the more complex and unique the personality. Pigs have nerve memory but their construction kits are simpler than ours; they have not remembered as much nor do they even have the capacity required for a critical-mass rollover into a higher state of genetic complexity., Keep pigs in the classroom from now till doomsday and they will still oink and roll in slime because *pig memory* is fixed in space and time and they are what genetic memory has molded for them.

You and I, though, have something very special going for us. The genetic memory that produces the human species came into the game *at* critical mass. It was a change of state that produced the first human. Genetic memory had reached an evolutionary barrier beyond which it could not travel, so it established a new baseline *beyond* the barrier, deposited its endowment over there with *something new* in terrestrial existence, an entirely new mold: the planetary experience of the ages became distilled in a new genetic system—a new packaging, like "hot dogs"—with a vast reservoir for nerve memory *and self-conscious expression*. Memory thus becomes more than a record of mere experience; it is now enriched by reflection upon and interpretation of experience. Thus, understanding enters memory and influences the interpretation of future experience.

For the first time on this planet, then, with the advent of man, nerve memory became more important than genetic memory. That is because genetic memory produces species which interact only with their environment. Nerve memory produces a unique individual who interacts with existence itself, questions it, examines it, interprets it. Put another way, you could say that nerve memory at a certain state is the awakening of cosmos; it is the universe becoming aware of itself.

I appreciate your patience if you are still with me, not left back there somewhere among the hot dogs and flaming poodles. I have brought you through all this because we are shortly going to get into some really wild stuff in this case so I think it best that you have some preparation for that which is to follow.

What I am asking you to consider, if you are to enjoy this case as much as I did, is that there is more to man than meets the eye, that we occupy a really special parcel of existence, that there is virtually no inherent limit to the degree with which we may interact with cosmos. It is important that you have this understanding because I will be introducing you to men and women whom you may otherwise find difficult to understand.

Clara Boone could be one of these.

She has gone through quite a transformation from the befuddled old lady I met at the police station. I am beginning to revise my presumption as to how *old* seventy-five really is. She has let her hair down, literally, and it falls in beautifully shimmering silver waves almost to the waist. We stroll with bare feet through the cold Pacific surf; her eyes glisten with excitement and she leaps with a squeal to avoid the rollers. We tarry beside the tidal pools and she gives me a wondering look of sheer delight when an anemone sucks her fingertip.

Later she is quietly reflective but no less transformed as we toast marshmallows on the open deck and watch a spectacular Pacific sunset. When the sun goes down in California, so does the temperature, abruptly; Clara shivers slightly and leans against me for warmth and it is good.

We go inside and build a fire. It is our only light and as we toast the night with red wine I no longer am aware of the wrinkled and sagging skin. I am experiencing the person, not her spatial envelope; there is a sense of timelessness and timeless memories hovering at the lip of awareness but we do not speak of these. I am man and she is woman but we cannot split the years between us, not in this envelope of time, and indeed neither of us wish to do so. It is enough that we are there at the same moment, to watch the flames consume the darkness and to shiver together with the knowledge that unrevealed memories tremble together between us.

If this sounds perverse to some then so be it, but we made a sort of love there without a touch and without a look, without a word between us. She arose as the final embers were flaring, touched my face lightly with the fingertips of both hands, and told me goodnight.

"Tomorrow I will tell you what you need to know," she said to me from the doorway to her bedroom.

"Clara," I replied, "God himself could not tell me what I need to know."

"God *her*self," she corrected me, and closed the door.

"Whatever," I said to the fireplace.

But I had just had one hell of a religious experience. And I knew that the best was yet to come.

CHAPTER
SEVEN

A Long
and Distant Journey

Clara awakened me at seven o'clock with breakfast on the table. I sat down to mouth-watering scratch biscuits and scrambled eggs and thoroughly enjoyed the meal. But Clara was seventy-five again. She was absentminded, sometimes confused, and did not seem to exactly understand where she was or why. Her legs ached and she was terribly worried about her birds and who was going to feed them. So I asked if she wanted me to take her home and it was obviously the right thing to say; it made her day.

I first told her that David Carver had died in the accident and I warned her that it could be awhile before the police released her car and/or continued her driving privileges. I also warned her about the press. She exhibited only a momentary sadness over Carver's death but was really upset about the car. I promised to look into the problem for her but this did little to allay her distress.

"I could walk to my birds," she said tremulously, "but how would I ever get to my sittings without my car?"

"What sittings?" I wanted to know.

"I have life sittings every Tuesday and Friday," she replied. "And I simply must have my car."

So I called Paul Stewart and asked him to massage the bureaucracy and get the car *delivered* to Clara without delay. He almost grudgingly agreed to do that. He also wondered if I was onto anything yet. I told him yeah, that I'd picked up a promising tremor or two and that I would keep him informed.

Enroute to Eagle Rock with Clara, I wanted to pursue that business about the life sittings.

Didn't bother her a bit. Apparently she had no secrets. "It's like memoirs," she told me. "Life to life."

"Life to life?"

"Yes. At my age, you see, this is very important. I am preparing for the next one."

"The next what, Clara?"

"The next life, of course. Isn't that what we are talking about?"

Okay. Sure. "How do you go about preparing for that?"

"We review. That will speed things up later."

"What things?"

"The selection of the next life. You are a grown man, my dear. Isn't it time you started thinking about your true self?"

I always thought I did. But maybe not. I told her, "Guess I've always been too enmeshed in the present life, Clara."

"Well that's the problem, you see. We all do that. And then we never really know where we are or who we are."

I said, "I'm Ashton Ford, Planet Earth, Citizen First Class. Who are you?"

That tickled her. She replied, "I was born this time as Clara Boone. But you must understand, this was not the first borning. And I certainly hope it shall not be the last."

We were talking reincarnation. I have always had an open mind on the subject but very mixed feelings about the aesthetics of the idea.

I said, "So this *review* is uh . . ."

"An attempt to see the present life in its proper relation to previous lives. Have I continued the growth plan or have I veered away? What must I do in the next life to stay on the track or to get back on it?"

"Uh huh. And you think that by doing this now . . ."

"My dear Mr. Ford, you must recognize that I am a very old woman. How much longer could I have? And if I die confused . . . well, I shall very probably take that confusion with me. It could take me eons to find my way back to the proper life."

I am aware that the idea of recurring lives in this same system sounds crack-brained to many people. But it is an idea that has been with us since prehistory, and it has been entertained or embraced by some of our greatest minds. Virtually every primitive culture has some version of reincarnation at the center of its religious thinking. It is a global idea, existing wherever mankind is, throughout Africa and Asia, Europe and America, in all the island nations, wherever man has paused to wonder about his origins and his fate, seeping into his art and literature, his sciences and philosophies. Longfellow's famous *Song of Hiawatha* embraces the idea in the farewell speech:

> I am going, O my people,
> On a long and distant journey;
> Many moons and many winters
> Will have come, and will have vanished,
> Ere I come again to see you.

Hiawatha was an actual figure. He was also known as Manabhozho and was a messianic figure for the Indians who expected him to return to life at some time with great power over the final fate of humankind. The speech quoted is a dying farewell, in almost the same spirit as Jesus at the Last Supper and Kahlil Gibran's *Prophet*.

Though once thought to be an idea peculiar to certain Asian religions, modern scholars have discovered that the idea had wide currency throughout early America, both north and south, and even the Eskimos have a reincarnation tradition. Similarly, the ancients of Europe—from Scandinavia to Italy—believed in reincarnation and the idea persisted into the Christian era. Indeed, scholars can point to many examples of early Christian and Jewish thought centering on rebirth, also among the Greeks and Romans—most notably Heraclitus, Herodotus, Socrates and Plato, Aristotle, Cicero, Lucretius, Ovid and Vergil, even the Emperor Julian.

But that's all primitive shit, you say—enlightened people of this modern age cannot be expected to swallow that stuff.

Well maybe not, but here are a few who have tasted it: Joseph Addison, Louisa May Alcott, Hervey Allen, Honoré de Balzac, James M. Barrie, Arnold Bennett, William Blake, Johann Ehlert Bode, Napoleon Bonaparte, Bernard Bosanquet, Francis Bowen, Sir Thomas Browne, Robert Browning, Pearl S. Buck, Sir Edward Bulwer-Lytton, Luther Burbank, Samuel Butler, Tomasso Campanella, Thomas Carlyle, Edward Carpenter, Edgar Cayce, Gina Cerminara, James Freeman Clarke, Samuel T. Coleridge, Sir Humphrey Davy, Charles Dickens, Emily Dickinson, John Donne, Feodor Dostoevsky, Lord Hugh Dowding, Arthur Conan Doyle, John Dryden, Thomas Edison, T. S. Eliot, Queen Elizabeth of Austria, Ralph Waldo Emerson, Henry Fielding, Gustave Flaubert, Henry Ford, Benjamin Franklin, Frederick the Great, Robert Frost, Mohandas K. Gandhi, Paul Gauguin, David Lloyd George, J.W. von Goethe, G. W. F. Hegel, Heinrich Heine, Herman Hesse, Oliver Wendell Holmes, Victor Hugo, David Hume, Aldous Huxley, Julian Huxley, Thomas H. Huxley, Henrik Ibsen, William James, Mary Johnston, James Jones, James Joyce, Carl G. Jung, Immanuel Kant, Søren Kierkegaard, Rudyard Kipling, Joseph Wood Krutch, G. W. Leibniz, D.H. Lawrence, Pierre Leroux, G.E. Lessing, John Leyden, Charles A. Lindbergh, Jack London, Henry Wadsworth Longfellow, Maurice Maeterlinck, Gustav Mahler, Norman Mailer, John Masefield, Somerset Maugham, Herman Melville, Henry Miller, John Milton, Friedrich Nietzsche, Eugene O'Neill, Edgar Allan Poe, J.B. Priestley, Ernest Renan, Jean Paul Richter, Rainer Maria Rilke, J. D. Salinger, George Sand, Friedrich Schiller, Friedrich von Schlegel, Arthur Schopenhauer, Sir Walter Scott, Ernest Thompson Seton (founder of Boy Scouts of America), William Shakespeare, George Bernard

Shaw, Percy Bysshe Shelley, Robert Southey, Edmund Spenser, Benedict Spinoza, Robert Stroud (Birdman of Alcatraz), Alfred Lord Tennyson, Henry David Thoreau, Leo Tolstoy, Voltaire, Richard Wagner, Walt Whitman, John Greenleaf Whittier, Thomas Wolfe, William Wordsworth, William Butler Yeats . . .

I go to all this trouble for Clara's sake, to put her in good company in your mind. She is really a sweet and sincere lady and does not appear at all kooky except in this single respect. Thomas Carlyle once wrote, "Every new opinion, at its starting, is precisely in a minority of one." That "minority of one" may always seem kooky to the rest of us. But 'taint necessarily so. As with Clara. She complains again of her legs then asks me, "Did she walk me a lot yesterday or something?"

I said, a bit startled by the question, "What?"

"What did you and Selma do while I was gone?"

"Selma?"

"Yes. My cosmic self. Didn't you know she was here?"

I had not known that, no—or had I? I told Clara, "We walked on the beach. Don't you remember? Later we toasted marshmallows above the breakers then relaxed in front of the fireplace. Don't you remember any of that?"

Clara replied in all sobriety, "No, I wasn't here for any of that. That's why my legs hurt. Selma always walks them off."

I thought about that for a couple of minutes, then asked her, "Exactly what is a cosmic self?"

"Selma is the real me," is the way she put it.

"And where is Selma when she is not here?"

"Oh she's always here but—you know—just sort of looking and listening."

"Have you ever talked directly with her, Clara?"

"Well yes, of course, that is what the life sittings are all about."

I said, "Uh huh. Is there a medium involved? Is this like a séance?"

"No no." She giggled. "Heavens, I don't commune with spirits. We just all sort of get together and start talking. You see, my circle is composed of fellow pilgrims."

"What does that mean?" I asked warily.

"Cosmic clusters. We began together, you see. Long ago. And we always manage to stick close together on earth. Well, that is, we try to." She made a sorrowful face. "Sometimes it takes most of a lifetime to get all the pilgrims together in recognition of one another."

I said, "I see," but I did not see.

I did, though, get an idea.

"Was Maybelle one of your pilgrims?"

"Yes indeed."

"A man named McSweeney?"

"Yes. Poor George suffered a terrible regression this time. He'll do better next time."

"Milhaul?"

"How did you know this?"

"Maybe I got it from Selma," I replied grimly. "Was Milhaul one of your group?"

She said with a quiet sigh, "That's right, that's right. Poor soul. I had forgotten. That is what your Mr. Carver came to talk to me about yesterday. Poor Esther."

I was getting very confused. "Who is Esther, Clara?"

"Well you see, that is—you see . . . Herman Milhaul was in a terrible pickle. Esther is Herman's cosmic self. And

Esther was very uncomfortable with Herman's present body."

I said, "Damn."

"Nobody is ever really damned," Clara gently advised me. "It may seem that way sometimes but . . . well, we just need to look to the next horizon."

We were approaching her house and I had the strongest feeling that I would not be talking with Clara again, ever. I pulled into her drive and went around to open the door for her; our gazes clashed and I had that shivery feeling again and I heard myself saying, "Thank you for last night, Selma."

Selma or Clara or someone replied, "Oh thank *you*, Ashton."

Clara, you see, always called me Mr. Ford.

And it was Clara who struggled from the car and onto her feet, wincing with the discomfort in those tired old legs. But I had to ask her one more.

"Is Reverend Annie one of your pilgrims?"

"Who?"

"Ann Farrel, pastor of the Church of the Light."

"Oh, you mean Ann Marie. Maybelle's daughter. No, no —heavens, I don't know about that girl. Sometimes I wonder if—never mind, never mind. I always say if you can't speak well of a person then you should not speak at all."

The subject was obviously closed. I walked Clara to her front door, kissed her on the cheek, and got the hell away from there.

I had about ten thousand questions trembling at the front of my brain but not tongue enough to utter a single one. And I did not know where the hell to go from there.

CHAPTER EIGHT

Life at the Surface of the Planet

Possibly I had stumbled onto the "tie" that David Carver was looking for when he died. If so, then, it was a very untidy package and the string was running everywhere. Clara had seemed very emphatic that Reverend Annie was not involved in the group of pilgrims, which however did include three of those who had died. If it was true that the late Maybelle Turner was Annie's mother, then there was a tie of sorts—and the fact that Milhaul and McSweeney were tied both to the pilgrims and to the Church of Light, if true, provided another loop to the knot. Certainly Reverend Annie appeared to be the common denominator in all of that, but I was not ready to leap to that conclusion, not yet.

Had Carver become entangled in that string? Or was his death exactly what it appeared to be, a grisly but innocent misfortune which could befall anyone anywhere?

And what about Annie's unfortunate past? Could any woman get that unlucky in love—four times a widow? Of course she could, any woman could. Just because it does not happen to all the people all the time does not mean that it cannot happen. It does happen.

So what did I really have?

Hell, I had nothing except some unlucky people, some very unfortunate people, and some kooky people. You can get that mix/match anywhere you go. What I actually had was a cop's gut suspicion . . . and those have been known to be fallible.

Also, of course, I had a nervous financier with possibly an overactive imagination and the means to go to any idiot length to protect an investment.

So I found myself tilting toward disengagement. I had other things to do with my time and I really did not have a sponsor here anyway. That is about where I was at in my head—the rest of me sort of drifting toward the Beverly Hills Hotel and lunch at the Polo Lounge—when the car phone rang and I received another summons from François. He wanted me to "come quickly" to his offices in Century City. It is very difficult to say no to François, especially when he is in an emotional state, and I was only a few minutes away from there anyway when the call came. So I dropped on down to Avenue of the Stars in Century City and left my Maserati at the Century Plaza Hotel—because I won't leave that car just anywhere and I like their valet service. The plaza is a small city within a city—though a very uptown small city with one of the area's plushest hotels, dozens of shops and restaurants, theaters, Playboy Club, the ABC Entertainment Center, and of course the Towers, twin monolithic high-rise office buildings, site of the suite of offices maintained by the incredible François. Not too long ago, the whole thing was part of the 20th-Century Fox back lot. Now it is about as uptown as you will get in Southern California, Beverly Hills notwithstanding.

I hoofed it across from the hotel to the towers via several different escalators and stairways—it's no small distance and the plaza is multilevel—then straight up like an arrow via express elevator to a point beyond sanity along the San Andreas fault. I like to think of myself as a sophisticated modern but I still believe that any structure above a hundred feet in earthquake country is the height of folly and no pun intended. So I wanted to make this visit quick and clean but that was not in the cards.

I went in past bubbling fountains and Corinthian leathers and hopeful startlets masquerading as receptionists to find François buried in a turret of video-phone monitors and in conference with the financial centers of Europe. He waved me to a chair and went on uninterrupted with dialogues in several languages but none in English. I had been there before. I went on back to the bar and helped myself to a drink then took a chair at the windows overlooking Century Park East which was much too far below. Heights have never bothered me except in California where it is particularly unnerving to be seated at a wall of glass hundreds of feet above a very unsteady earth. But there was no place else to sit so I repositioned the chair with my back to all that and tried to relax with bourbon while François bought and sold Europe.

I was building my second relaxer when François joined me at the bar. He poured a thimble of Cognac into a snifter,

sampled it with his nose, then told me without further pre-
amble, "Our Annie is in trouble."

I said, "No!" very sarcastically, I'm afraid.

"But yes. Even now she is with the police. I have send my
best lawyers to guarantee her rights but this yet could be not
enough. Do you have influence at the police?"

I replied, "None I've ever noticed. Has she been arrested?"

He gave me an exasperated look and said, "Arrested or
not arrested makes no difference. Merely the hint of wrong-
doing is enough to ruin her. Can you stop this?"

I said, "I don't know what to stop or where, François.
Settle down and tell me what's going on."

He belted the Cognac without removing his gaze from
mine. "Going is this Lieutenant Stewart at the Gestapo. He
orders that she present herself for questioning. So I have
send my best lawyers with her to make sure she is not vio-
lated. But still I worry."

"Questioning about what?"

He shrugged. "What is the difference? To be questioned is
to presume guilt, is it not? There must be no hint—"

I growled, "Cut the shit, François. What is Stewart talking to her about?"

His gaze fell away as he replied, "He is suspicious about
the deaths."

I said, "Well hooray, so are a lot of people. But does
Stewart *have* anything?"

"This I do not know."

"Look at me, dammit. *Could* he have anything?"

He looked at me but then the eyes flicked away again as
he said, "What does it matter? I wish it saved, Ashton."

I said, "Go straight to hell, François. I don't work that way and you know it."

He knew it, yeah, and I guess that was the only reason he tolerated me. I wouldn't kiss his ass but he knew I wouldn't kiss any others, either. I think he respected that. But a tic began working at his left eye as he quietly told me, "The investment is in millions already. It is secured for her the satellite channels for worldwide broadcast, interpreters in a hundred tongues, a ministry of the entire world and all will love her. You must help us realize this, Ashton."

I honestly could not have said at that moment whether the guy was asking me to help him con the world or to save it. So I put it directly to him. "What are your projected first-year profits?"

He smiled, lit a cigarette, went to the window, turned back to me with a sparkle in the eyes. "I will have the profits, yes, but Annie will have the dream."

"What dream is that?"

The sparkle turned to a snap as he said, "What is this inquisition, Ashton? And what is this absurd naiveté? Tell me what has moved this world into the modern age, my friend. Is it altruism or personal incentive?—nationalism or commerce? Has the religion made your America the greatest power of all times?"

I was beginning to suspect that the guy had been conning me all these years or else he'd taken a crash language course since our last meeting. I was suddenly understanding every word he said. I told him, "A strong dollar has helped."

"But of course. It has helped also the religion in America. Has it not?"

I said, "The comic, Lenny Bruce, had a line I always

liked. He said to show him a preacher with two suits of clothes while another man had no clothes at all and he'd show you a con man."

François chuckled and extinguished his cigarette. "Did Lenny Bruce perform for free?"

"Not if he could help it, I guess," I conceded.

"So did not he too profit from religion? Do the police not profit from crime? And does the priest not profit from sin?"

He had a point there. I just was not sure how it applied but I conceded it. "You have a point there."

"Ah yes. So how does it matter what drives the engine if all the passengers arrive at their destination, eh?"

I told him, "A countryman of yours had something to say about that. Guy name La Rochefoucald. Heard of him?"

"To be sure. A namesake. He too was a François."

I said, "Yeah. More of a moralist than you, though. He wrote three hundred years ago that no action, no matter how brilliant, is to be considered great unless it is the result of a great motive."

My François shrugged and replied with only a trace of accent, "You speak of greatness while I speak of life at the surface of the planet. The masses do not feed on greatness, Ashton, and even the priests have known this from the beginning. This is why they feed the masses chants and rituals while confining the holy mysteries within locked vaults. So do not moralize with me on the virtues of virtue itself. And do not ask me to engage your virtue. I engage your talent, Ashton. Only that has accuracy in this world of commerce. Do not be confused."

I was not at all confused. Not at the moment, anyway. I told François, "Okay, maybe I'll sell you some talent—but you'll have to take my idea of virtue in the package—and also on one very large condition."

"What is the condition?" he asked with a smile.

"That you don't lay the phony accent on me ever again."

He went right on smiling and replied, "Very well, but you must honor the secret. It is, after all, often a valuable advantage this ability to dissimulate."

I knew that, yes. And I had to wonder if that ability to dissimulate extended beyond language into more subtle nuances of human intercourse. The guy had a lot more depth than any he'd shown me in times gone by.

Frankly, I was intrigued by this new François. But that is not why I changed my mind about disengagement.

I changed my mind because Annie joined us near the end of that conversation and she was obviously in deep difficulty.

Well, she sort of joined us but only I knew that. I saw her reflection in the window glass behind François while he was expounding on greatness and the needs of the masses. I say reflection even though she could not have been standing outside, and yet that could not accurately describe what I saw because a window glass cannot reflect that which is not physically present, can it?

However and wherever, I saw Annie and I knew that she was in high distress. She was asking for help. Not from François but from me. I could hardly disengage at that point.

So I advised François to stick close to the telephone and I made a quick departure. I called Stewart from the Maserati and he confirmed that the lady had a problem.

"We are getting ready to book her," he told me. "The charge is murder one. Three times."

I don't know why it shocked me so. I croaked, "Three counts?"

"Right," the cop replied. "And that is just the beginning."

It was just the beginning for me too. I should have disengaged right there.

CHAPTER NINE

A View with Prejudice

Apparently Paul Stewart had found a direction for his anger over David Carver's death. By the time I got downtown Annie had already been hustled off to Sybil Brand, the local lockup for women, and her lawyers were scratching at judicial doors for her quick release pending a formal hearing.

Stewart had the easy, relaxed look of a man who knows he's right but there were flaws in that self-satisfaction, small tremors of doubt here and there that were evidenced by the body language as he outlined the case to me. I was a bit surprised to discover that the deaths charged against Annie were not the latest three in the series close to her but the deaths of three of her husbands. And though it was comforting to learn that all of the evidence in the case was purely circumstantial, it was a bit distressing to see that an imaginative prosecutor could weave it all together in a damning indictment.

"That woman is a black widow," Stewart said confidently. "And a very clever one, at that. The insurance companies paid off on each one without a murmur but it was the last one that undid her—the last insurance company, I mean. They paid, sure, but one of their investigators began having second thoughts several months ago, after learning about the first two. I turned the guy over to Carver—we get a lot of that. By and large any insurance company hates like hell to pay off on any policy, so they'll go after any little hook they can find to get out of it. So we get a lot of private investigators crawling through here and you can't take them all seriously. I palmed the guy off on Carver. I think our black widow intrigued him, really got into his belly. The more he looked at her the more he began to see the outlines of the red hourglass on her underside. He came in here two or three times a week every week for the past two months wanting to bring charges but hell . . ."

"You weren't buying it."

"Nothing to buy," Stewart said, with a giveaway twitch of the lip. He massaged the back of his hand and went on. "But he kept digging. And he found a sympathetic ear at the D.A.'s office. The Milhaul thing was the log that broke the jam. Just yesterday the D.A. decided to take the thing to the grand jury. David did not live to see that development." His eyes fell, then came back hard and demanding on mine. "But now I want you to tell me something—and I don't want a lot of hedging and double-talking when you tell me. Is there a way to project psychic power? And could that woman be doing something like that?"

I said, "You're thinking of Carver's death."

"Bet your ass I am," he shot back.

"Your answer is yes," I said, sighing. "But you'd never prove it in a court of law."

"Has it ever been scientifically validated? I mean, under carefully controlled laboratory conditions?"

"Yes, it has," I replied, "but not everyone in the scientific community believes it. It's a very difficult thing to nail down conclusively. So there's always an angle of attack for those who feel compelled to attack such things. Your problem, I think, would be to conclusively prove that *Annie* has that kind of power."

"That's where you're wrong," he said. "The woman *claims* that kind of power. We can fix her on her own petard if I can get twelve men and women to buy a reasonable presumption that it *is* possible, that Ann Farrel *has* it, and that by God she's been using it."

I muttered, "Shades of Salem."

He said, "Come on. I—"

I said, "You come on. Do you actually have someone at the D.A.'s office who's willing to take on—"

"No I haven't," the cop said angrily. "But she did it to her husbands the old-fashioned way. We'll prove it, and that establishes her character. She is willing to kill. Okay. I want a by-God presumption working in our favor to say that she's found a neater way to kill, a safer way, and that she has killed at least four more times that way. I'll get it, too."

I said, "Well, for what it's worth, I think you could be right. Not that you *are*, especially, but that you could be. Your problem will be to find respectable expert witnesses to back you up in court."

"You think that might be a problem?"

I told him, "I know it will be a problem."

He studied my face for a moment, then asked, "What about you?"

"I said *respectable*," I replied. "I have no credentials to present to a court. I really feel obligated to advise you against this. How many times can she swing? If you've already got—"

"I'll keep in touch," he said sullenly, ending the debate. "You do that too. And let me know if something develops for you."

I said, "I need to tell you that I have been asked to enter the case in her defense."

Stewart snapped me a hard look. "Who asked?"

I told him, "She did."

"Going to do it?"

I said, "I'm already in it. To my ears. Guess I'll stick around to see how it falls. You can cancel my voucher. I didn't turn anything for you. But I will keep in touch."

He stopped me at the door and turned me back with a harsh aftershot. "We have a saying around here, Ford."

"And that is . . .?"

"If you're not for us, you're against us."

So I gave him mine. "If truth be for you, why then fear the false witness?"

He snickered and replied, "I'm not afraid of you."

I said, "No reason you should be. Unless . . ."

He scowled. "Unless what?"

"Unless I can project too."

He lost a couple of beats before replying. "Can you?"

"Anybody can," I told him, and went on out.

So maybe I'd made an enemy. But not nearly so emphatically as had Reverend Annie. This just did not seem like the Paul Stewart I'd always known. It was as though all of

David Carver's guts had been transplanted into his boss and done so with rage and vindictive purpose. So maybe there really was a case against Annie and maybe not.

You tell me.

Here is what Stewart had.

Annie's second husband was a Donald Huntzerman. He was sixty, a successful retail merchant, she was twenty-one and working as a cocktail waitress when they met. Huntzerman had already suffered two heart attacks and was under close medical supervision when they married. He owned a $100,000 life insurance policy which had been written many years before his heart condition became evident. He bought Annie a new home in an exclusive neighborhood and made her the beneficiary of his insurance, but all other assets he brought into the marriage were set aside by will for his grown children by two previous marriages.

Huntzerman's family regarded Annie as a fortune hunter. Why else would a beautiful girl marry a sick man three times her age? Others, though, noted that the pair always seemed very happy and in love, and Annie apparently devoted herself to his care. He had several moderate attacks requiring hospitalization during the first two years, then died of a massive hit just two months short of their third anniversary.

Annie wore widow's black for precisely thirty days, then sold the house, collected the life insurance, and took a world tour. Carver dug up a guy who signed an affidavit to the effect that Ann Huntzerman paid his expenses to Paris and Rome then abandoned him without funds or a return ticket home. Another affidavit was signed by a mortician's assistant asserting that "it took all our skill" to properly prepare the deceased for burial services due to "numerous lesions about the throat and wrists. It looked like this man had been kept tied like a dog."

For the record, Carver also had a statement from a nurse who provided live-in care for Huntzerman, to the effect that her patient "tended to claw at" the intravenous tubes which were attached at his arms throughout the final two months of life. "We had to tie his wrists to the bed," she stated.

That is the whole file on Huntzerman, as provided by Paul Stewart.

The next "victim" was Larry Preston, a forty-year-old dry cleaner with a chain of stores situated along the San Fernando Valley—mostly coin-operated but he also had a very modern plant in North Hollywood and one in Encino. According to David Carver's information, Ann Huntzerman was broke and looking for work when she met Preston. They were married ten days later and husband number three died almost exactly one year after that when his service truck blew up on the Ventura Freeway. The official investigation at the time blamed escaping naphtha from a damaged container in the rear of the truck. During his own investigation, Carver secured a statement from a man who had been employed by Preston denying that the container had been damaged. The employee stated that he had personally inspected the container and placed it in the truck shortly before it exploded.

Again Annie came into a bit of money but she had to fight for it. An ex-wife raised a claim and it took two years to get the estate through probate.

She was apparently broke again, though, when she married George Farrel, a respected cinematographer with a number of Oscar nominations in his list of credits. Again, he was considerably older but she was narrowing those gaps through her own maturation; Annie was now thirty-one, George was sixty-two. He retired several months after the marriage and they spent a year touring the West in a motor home. Then they took delivery on a new Mercedes in Europe and toured the Continent for another year. The third and final year of the marriage was spent in Southern California in George's home of thirty years, a modest house in a modest neighborhood in Van Nuys, and neighbors interviewed later by David Carver unanimously agreed that "something was wrong" during that entire period. Apparently Farrel had always been a gregarious and cheerful neighbor through the years; now he hardly ever showed himself outside the house except at night and would turn away without response when someone spotted and greeted him.

One woman signed a lengthy and rambling affidavit stating that several times she had been turned away at the door by Ann Farrel, always with the excuse that "George isn't feeling well." Number Four died from a fall in his bathtub, near the end of that third year. According to the official record, Annie had maintained a constant vigil at his hospital bed night and day for three months then pulled the plug when her husband was certified brain dead. A statement from a hospital worker, elicited by Carver, claims that Annie exerted constant and extreme pressure upon the board of physicians to get that certification.

Farrel's estate cleared out at just under $200,000. He had executed a new will earlier that year leaving all to his widow although he acknowledged an adult son born out of wedlock.

That is the whole ball of wax, as revealed to me by Lt. Stewart. Is this a portrait of evil, or what?

I did not know what the hell to think about it.

But I have always been slow to move squarely onto a

point of view without wondering how it would look from another angle. I wanted to hear Annie's own version of the Ann Farrel story, and I wanted to do some checking around on my own.

I also wanted another talk with Bruce Janulski, Annie's personal secretary.

Because Bruce, you see, the gentle Adonis, was George Farrel's illegitimate son. And that was a tie that Carver had apparently missed, or else he chose to ignore it. Either way, I wanted to know why.

CHAPTER
TEN

From the Shadows of the Mind

I went looking for Janulski at church headquarters. It was very nice the way they'd taken a decaying little shopping mall and converted it into a spiritual center. Book and gift shops, classrooms, reading rooms, a lecture hall, the church itself which had previously served as a small supermarket, a chapel, personal quarters for Annie though she did not actually live there, and a surprisingly upscale suite of offices. Someone had also done some remarkable landscaping that did not seem typical of a retail trade center. A quick scan of the scheduled activities posted on a bulletin board out front indicated that The Spiritual Center of Light was a very busy place indeed, seven days a week, with fully a dozen or more consciousness-raising events every day—even to weekend musical concerts and "sings." My eyebrows rose at the scheduled performances for the upcoming weekend; she could have booked those shows into the Dorothy Chandler Pavilion or the Greek and made a bundle. Or maybe she made a bundle anyway, if these people performed for free.

I found the gentle Adonis in the chapel fussing with a floral arrangement on the altar. He looked up with a shy smile that grew as he recognized me and came forward to greet me.

"Mr. Ford, how wonderful," he said warmly.

This guy was so sweet he might melt if he got wet. But it seemed genuine if nothing else and I could not help but respond to that. I took him by the arm and walked him toward the door as I asked him, "Have you heard from your boss today?"

He replied, "Well no, I have not, but she told me last night—" his voice softened almost to a whisper "—that she might go into retreat for a few days. But if there is anything at all that I can do for you, I am certainly at your service."

I matched his own quiet tone as I told him, "Me, you can't help, Bruce—her, maybe so. She needs all the help she can get right now."

He batted his eyes at me and said, "I certainly agree with that."

I steered him to an invitingly shaded gazebo just outside the chapel and suggested that he sit down. He did so, crossed his ankles, placed both hands in his lap palms up, showed me a level stare. "You are preparing me for some awful news," he said quietly.

"Yes," I said. "Annie's in jail. She's been charged with

three counts of murder. But François Mirabel's attorneys are with her so I expect her to be released on bail very quickly."

The blood drained from his face. He whispered, "Good lord!" and raised both hands to his cheeks.

That told me what I really wanted to know, first off; namely that he genuinely cared for the lady. Otherwise I wanted to be his agent because a scene like that one was Oscar material. I began to think I was going to have to thump him on his back or something because all the breath had left him and none was coming back in for the longest time. Finally he caught it with a sob and tears began oozing from his eyes.

I said, "Hey, it'll be okay."

He grabbed a handkerchief and went after the tears while he told me, "I'm sure that it will be, Mr. Ford, thank you. It's just that I have been arrested too, and let me tell you it is not a pleasant experience. I cannot bear the thought of her being subjected to such indignities. Oh my God!"

"What?"

"The strip search! Did they do that to her?"

I said, "I think it's one of the routines, Bruce."

Funny thing, there. He didn't even want to know who'd been murdered or why Annie had been charged. He was just totally focused on . . .

"They give that job to the perverts, you know. I suppose with a woman they even violate her vagina."

I said, "I don't believe so. You're thinking of drug searches and—"

"No, no, what do you think they're looking for in jail?"

At least the tears had stopped flowing. I told him, "Whatever, Bruce, Annie can handle it. She *is* handling it. But we have to—"

"I'll just confess to the murders myself," he said, giving me an up-and-down look. "I won't let them drag her through that."

I said, "If you're going to do that, don't you want to know who it is you killed?"

"Do you detest me, Mr. Ford?"

It was my turn to give him the up and down. Actually the question was from so far out in left field that it took me a moment to assimilate it. I replied to that, "Why the hell should I detest you? I barely know you."

"Yes, but you knew immediately that I am gay, and don't deny it. I saw it in your face the other night. It was just as obvious to me, you know, that you are straight. But I don't detest you for that."

I didn't know why he went for my throat that way and at that particular moment, but he'd caught me with my buried prejudices exposed and twisting slowly in the wind—and, yes, I was feeling just a tad defensive when I told him, "To each his own, pal, has always been my motto. I don't ask anybody what they do behind closed doors and furthermore I don't give a damn what they do."

"Yes, but you still see gayness as a sexual perversion. Don't deny it."

I told him, very patiently, "I do deny it—but I resent being called upon to do so. Actually I think that celibacy is the only perversion of the sexual instinct. To paraphrase a popular song of some years ago, the music goes round and round and it comes out wherever it can. So long as it comes out, okay. Okay?"

I guess it was not okay.

"You miss the entire point, Mr. Ford. Will you please look at me? Look at me! What you see is what I am. I am not having sex with anybody right now. As far as you know, I have never had sex and maybe I never will. So what are you looking at? What are you seeing?"

I tried again. "Bruce, I see a very sweet guy who acts for all the world like a very sweet girl. Maybe that puts me off just a bit. But I think none the less of you."

"Oh really?" He was giving me the arched-eyebrow gaze. "Then why do you talk to me like I'm some kind of idiot? Why do you patronize me?"

I said, "How do you know I don't treat everyone the same way?" Hell, maybe I did.

He flexed those tremendous shoulders and told me, "I could break you in two if I wanted to."

I mildly warned him, "Don't try. You could get surprised. Anyway, why would you want to? How have I hurt you?"

"You haven't hurt me, Mr. Ford," he replied. "But you and I need some very serious conversation and I want to be sure that our minds are connecting when we do. I don't want you to think of me as an idiot and I do not want you patronizing me."

I thought about that for several seconds then told him, "Okay, maybe you're right. I apologize if I've come at you that way. I would not consciously do that. So maybe there is something down in the subconscious that—"

"There certainly is," he said, interrupting my apology with a solemn smile. "A moment ago you said that I act like a very sweet girl. That tells a lot about the way you've been conditioned to think about people like me. I am not a girl, you see, and I would not want to be a girl. Also, however, I am not a boy . . . and I would not want to be a boy. Your understanding of these distinctions could be crucial to your understanding of Reverend Annie's difficulties. Frankly I was very surprised when the guides recommended you. I mean, after I found out who you are, and all."

I said, "Speaking of Reverend Annie . . ."

He responded in that same solemn manner. "Oh, yes, I know, you think I'm being very silly carrying on this way at such a time. But you see I've been expecting just such a complication. It always works that way."

"What do you mean? What always works which way?"

He rearranged his legs, smoothed his trousers, said, "Well, that is precisely what we need to be talking about. And I just want to be sure that you will respect what I have to tell you."

I assured him, "I am not trying to amuse myself with meaningless games, Bruce. So let me level with you first. It appears that I have been drawn into this thing without my conscious knowledge or consent. I have been pushed one way and pulled another to the point that I'm a bit confused as to where the flow is even coming from."

Janulski nodded quiet agreement, whispered, "Yes, that's the way it works."

"To the point that I am not sure that your Reverend Annie is deserving of help, especially my help. I am sensitive to unseen forces, however, and I am aware that events in this world are sometimes no more than a shadow play of events in another."

"Oh exactly, exactly."

"I won't guarantee you that I will remain sympathetic to Annie's problems once I understand them. But I do want to understand them. And I will want to help if I feel the cause is right."

"It is, believe me."

"On the other hand," I warned him, "if it turns the other way, it's possible that I would want to help the other side."

Janulski laughed prettily. "Believe me," he said, "you wouldn't like it over there."

We decided to move to Annie's office to continue the discussion. He offered refreshments as we passed through the reception area. I wanted coffee; he opted for tea and passed the request along to one of the women.

As we entered Annie's sanctum, Janulski lightly touched my shoulder and told me, "I have a delightful surprise for you."

I really did not want to know but I asked anyway, "What is that?"

He sat down behind the desk, put his hands together, and told me, "We are really not supposed to divulge information of this nature but it is just too perfect, so I've received special permission to tell you about it."

I took a chair at the opposite side of the desk and said, "Okay."

"Well, this is going to thrill you. One of my guides was your father in a previous life."

I did not feel especially thrilled. A bit creepy, maybe, but . . . I had no memory whatever of any father at any time. I said drily to Janulski, "Well, then, you must introduce us."

His eyes were twinkling as he replied, "I just might be able to do that."

Well, hell, that more or less set the tone for what was to follow. I give that to you, below, exactly as it developed.

You tell me what it was all about.

CHAPTER
ELEVEN

From the Mouths
of Angels

"If you are not a boy and not a girl, then what are you?"

"There, you see? You are right at the crux. There has never been any really original thought about this. In this world there are precisely two sexes and we all must fit into one or the other. May I tell you a secret? There are many more worlds than this one, and there are more sexes than two."

"Maybe so, but we all now have to deal with this world. So don't you have to declare yourself as one or the other, male or female?"

"Declaring doesn't make it so and certainly doesn't make it easier for those of us who are neither. All that does is satisfy a classification system designed for animals. Good heavens! Can't these twentieth-century minds understand that the human race has left the animal kingdom behind?"

"Not entirely behind. That body of yours, pal, which you say is neither boy nor girl, was created by an animalistic act that produces nothing but boys and girls."

"Oh, well, if you're talking about bodies ...! Bodies ...! good lord!... that's like saying there's nothing but fucking and sucking and no such thing as making love! I can fuck or suck anybody—understand? Anybody, boy or girl makes no difference, if you just want fucked or sucked. But if you want love from me, pure romantic love, then you have to be one of my own kind. You could fuck a cow, Mr. Ford. But could you fall in love with one?"

"Not sure I could fuck one, Bruce. But I guess I see what you mean. You couldn't fall in love with me?"

"Sorry, no, I could not. Oh, I can *love* you. I do love you. But not ... no, sorry."

"Don't feel bad. Just wanted to be sure I'm getting you. You are saying, like, you could not fall in love with Annie or—"

"Good heavens no!"

"—or with anyone else who is not one of these uh, this third sex or whatever—"

"Third sex, no, that's not accurate. It's like ummm, there's an island where people from all over the world vacation. They all seem very much alike but ummm, people from Europe are attracted to others from Europe, those from Asia go with Asians, and those from Africa go for Africans."

"Yes?"

"Well, ummm, I'm from Africa and I am nearly crazy looking for other Africans."

"You are telling me, Bruce . . ."

"Yes, I am telling you that we are different souls—a different order of souls trying to fit ourselves into this crazy world. Aliens, if you will, aliens . . . trying our best to find a fit where no fit is possible. Not possible, that is, the way the rules of the game have been rigged against us. It's like decreeing that no Africans may fall in love."

"That's an interesting concept."

"It's much more than a concept, I'm afraid. Luckily I have found the truth for myself. But for each one like me, there are thousands like poor Herman."

"You knew Herman, then? We're talking Herman Milhaul? Somehow I got the impression that you hadn't—when I mentioned his name the other night you acted dumb."

"I knew him vaguely. The name didn't ring a bell right away. I'd heard—but I could not help him. He was too lost, too confused, poor soul. Well, he's getting the dickens for it right now."

"Where uh, where is he getting that?"

"Another realm. He'll be given time to straighten it out, then he'll have to try again."

"He'll be born again?"

"Yes."

"Same as before?"

"Considering the record this last time, yes, I'm sure of it."

"You're saying he has no sexual choice."

"At this stage of his evolution, none whatever. He's been through all the rest and mastered it. Now he must master this."

"You mean that he has evolved into a gay soul?"

"That *is* an amusing idea. But it's not too far from the

truth, at that. For want of a better name here on earth, yes; I suppose you could think of him as a gay soul."

"Is there a name for it in that other realm?"

"Yes, there is. But there is no exact correspondence in our language. There is a word, however, that is very close."

"Which one is that?"

"Angel."

"Angel?"

"Close enough, yes. Close enough."

I must interrupt the transcript at this point because it is here that we begin to veer away into the other stuff and I wish, for the record (same as I did for Clara), to place Bruce into proper perspective. Here are just a few of the more familiar names of those who might sympathize most strongly with Bruce's struggle for understanding: Alexander the Great, Horatio Alger, Hans Christian Andersen, W. H. Auden, Edward II (English king), Gaius Julius Caesar, André Gide, Nikolai Gogol, Hadrian, Henry III (French king), Rock Hudson, Alexander von Humboldt, James I (English king), John Maynard Keynes, Leonardo da Vinci, W. Somerset Maugham, Michelangelo (Buonarroti), Montezuma II, Plato, Cole Porter, Marcel Proust, Richard I (the Lion-Hearted—English king), Arthur Rimbaud, Camille Saint-Saëns, Sappho, Pope Sixtus IV (Francesco della Rovere), Socrates, Sophocles, Gertrude Stein, Petr Ilich Tchaikovsky, Walt Whitman, Tennessee Williams . . .

Angels all, perhaps, if Bruce is right.

"How widely is it known, Bruce, that Annie is—how would you call it?—sort of like your stepmother."

"Who told you that?"

"I picked it up. Is it true?"

"It's a ridiculous thought. First off, she is only a few years older than I. Secondly, no man ever formally acknowledged fathering me; not to me, anyway. But if you are alluding to the fact that Annie married a man of advanced years who virtually on his death bed claimed to be my father, no, we do not talk about that."

"Have you ever discussed it with her?"

"Well of course I have. It was she who sought me out and brought me to his deathbed."

"I understood that he died from a fall in the bathtub."

"He died from injuries sustained in that fall. He was in his death coma when first I learned of him."

"So you never really had a chance to talk to him."

"It's just as well. I probably would have cursed him. I was not as enlightened then as I am now."

"How old are you, Bruce?"

"Well now, that is a rude question."

"Fuck it. How old are you?"

"I'm twenty-eight. How old are you?"

"Older than that, but not much. I never knew my dad either. Not even on his deathbed. My name is Ford by pure chance and my mother's wit. I was conceived on the backseat of one, you see. If she even knew his name she took the secret to the grave with her. But I don't believe I would curse him if I met him now."

"Obviously you had a more pleasant childhood than I did. I was regarded as a humiliating bastard all my life by grandparents who gave me their name but never their affection. My mother died while I was an infant. I did not know until just about a year ago that George Farrel paid support to my grandparents all the way through college. They never told me about him. Annie did, God love her. She wanted to unite us before he died. He was in quite bad health, you know, for more than a year before his accident."

"I didn't know that, no."

"Uh huh. Probably why he fell. She was at his side constantly but, you know, these things happen. Look away for just a second and that's all it takes. She was inconsolable for the longest time. Blamed herself. Why do we do that? That woman is a saint, but still she had to take the guilt."

"She also took the estate, though, didn't she."

"How dare you!"

"Sorry. I didn't mean—well yes, I guess I did. Let's be honest if nothing else. She got your dad's estate. You got nothing. How do you feel about that?"

"Look around you, Mr. Ford. *This* is my father's estate. It is no more Annie's than mine. We are both merely stewards."

"Nonprofit corporation?"

"Of course."

"Could I see your charter?"

"Any time. Ask one of the ladies."

"Are you an officer?"

"Of course. I am the executive vice-president. And I have a lifetime chair on the board of directors."

"Then what is all this jazz about Annie's personal secretary?"

"I am that, too."

"Uh huh. How 'bout the deal François Mirabel is cooking up? Do you have a piece of that?"

"Do *I* have? Not the personal *I*, of course not. But all net proceeds will go to the corporation. What are you suggesting?"

"Just curious. You said earlier that you have been expecting misfortune, that things work that way. What did you mean by that?"

"Well, I simply meant that the law has been set in motion."

"Which law is that?"

"The law of opposition. It is always there."

"Sort of like action and reaction?"

"Well yes, sort of, but more than that. Much more pervasive. For every force there is an opposing force. This dynamic tension is everywhere. It keeps things balanced. Say, for instance, you hurl a rock into the air. Why shouldn't it just keep on going, because actually it is falling away from the earth. But it returns very quickly to earth under the counterforce of gravity."

"I don't uh . . . see the connection, Bruce, between the law of gravity and what is happening to Reverend Annie."

"I said for instance, didn't I. Something very much like that happens any time any force is exerted upon the universe. Spiritual force as well as physical force. Any time you start pushing, something starts pushing back. It's the law."

"Are we talking good and evil?"

"Heavens no, it's all the same thing. We are talking force and counterforce, the dynamic balance in the universe. Good heavens, Ford, don't you understand that life itself is a force and that every other thing in the universe is opposing that force? That's the way it works. Not good or evil. Just simply the way it works. And things get *dreadfully* tense when a strongly spiritual force is present."

"A spiritual force such as Annie."

"Precisely. The entire universe must this moment be gathering its forces to annihilate her."

"That's uh . . . that's quite a presumption, isn't it? I mean, that the entire universe—we're talking time-space, right?—the whole time-space universe is getting nervous about the activities of a relatively infinitesimal speck on the planet Earth?"

"Snicker if you must. I'm telling you that is the way it works."

"Well thanks, Bruce, but I haven't had time to examine your credentials yet."

"A pox on credentials. They don't mean a thing. I wasted four precious years going to college to learn precisely nothing about anything worthwhile. A single night with my guides means more than all the universities combined could give me."

"Yeah, I wanted to ask you about them. What do these guys do other than hang around waiting for you to consult them?"

"You really do not respect my guides, do you."

"I didn't say that, Bruce."

"You don't have to say it, Ashton. By the way, I understand that you and Selma had a delightful time."

"What?"

"Selma? By the seashore? Come now. You haven't forgotten already."

"Bruce?"

"Yes, Ashton."

"Could I have a go at those guides of yours?"

"I will see what can be done."

"Soon, Bruce."

"There is a certain element of danger involved."

"I'll chance that."

"You will be opening yourself to influences that could, ah, alter your view of reality."

"I'll chance that too."

"Very well. I will try. You already have a friend in court, so . . ."

"Yeah. You mentioned him."

"He's an angel."

"An angel? You mean . . .?"

"A perfect angel, Ashton."

CHAPTER TWELVE

A Family Affair

We moved to a conference room and sat at opposite sides of a round mahogany table that was set for six. The chairs were heavy, comfortable, nicely spaced. A gooseneck microphone, a small pad, and a ballpoint pen were placed at each position.

The floor was carpeted wall to wall and the walls themselves were bare and shiny, unmarred except for a small air-conditioning vent at the rear. A rectangular skylight, about two by three feet, was emplaced in the ceiling directly above the table, providing good natural illumination. There were no windows. The microphones had no cords; each sprouted a tiny antenna. There was no PA system that I could detect, so I guessed radio mikes to an outside taping system.

I had hardly sat down before a man and two women came in and quietly positioned themselves at the table, the women together on my left side, the man between Janulski and me. They exchanged cordial greetings with Janulski, smilingly acknowledged introductions to me. All three were forty-ish.

Hilda was very pretty in a roundish Scandinavian way, blond hair thickly braided about her head, very little makeup.

Rachel was slender everywhere but in the chest, had evidently burned all her bras, wore her dark hair short and neatly styled; also very attractive.

Ted looked like a guy who'd spent his life at a desk—or maybe in a classroom—very smooth hands, an intelligent snap to the eyes, a quick laugh, entirely masculine.

There was nothing creepy or weird about any of these; altogether they were a comely and likable trio.

Janulski gave them no setup whatever. He merely pushed his pad and pen aside and said, "Let's get started."

Mind you, I have been to a séance or two and I guess I'm somewhat familiar with every mediumistic trick in the bag. This approach was decidedly different from anything I'd ever seen.

The room was well lighted. There were no props, no music, nothing at all to distract or to aid deception. It was a bare room except for table and chairs, not even a vase of flowers or a picture.

There was no mumbo jumbo, no wailings, no sighing or murmuring. The three mediums merely rested their hands atop the table with palms up, closed their eyes, bowed their heads, and announced almost in unison that they were ready.

Janulski then did likewise, maintained a silence of about ten seconds, then very softly announced, "We bring to your attention Ashton Ford, whom we discussed earlier. We ask that you recognize him and counsel him."

My attention was of course focused on Janulski. But within seconds, perhaps no more than five, Rachel stirred slightly and her throat began to flutter ever so gently in a very fast rhythmic pulsing.

At the same instant I became aware of a different quality to the atmosphere within that room—the physical atmosphere, that is, the air itself, almost a different *charge*—electrical charge, like on a hot summer day just before the thundershower—I could even smell it, like ozone—and I could *see* a fine thickening or whatever in the atmosphere immediately surrounding Rachel.

Ted got into the act then with identical behavior except that the thing with the throat was more pronounced, his Adam's apple sliding up and down rapidly like a guy guzzling a Coke.

Hilda was only a beat behind, and the atmosphere in that room had become strongly enough charged to lift the hairs on my arms.

Janulski opened his eyes and whispered, "Thank you for coming."

Rachel's mouth opened like a mechanical doll's and issued a single harshly whispered word: "Peril."

Janulski caught my eye and pointed to his notepad. So I casually picked up my ballpoint, not really overly impressed at that moment, but then hastened to catch up as the words began flying back and forth across that table.

Let me set it up for you properly so that I can dispense with all this description and just give you what was said. Hilda spoke second and then Ted, both exactly in the way I gave it to you for Rachel—just a single whispered word at a time—but in very quick succession and not necessarily in proper rotation.

Rachel: "Peril . . ."

Hilda: ". . . precedes . . ."

Ted: ". . . peace."

Hilda: "Sorrow . . ."

Ted: ". . . accompanies . . ."

Rachel: ". . . joy."

I thought at first they were giving me epigrams. Whatever, they were giving them damned fast. I had to use stroke codes to identify each speaker and still I was having a hell of a time keeping up. By about the third round, I even had to abandon the speaker code and just go for the words themselves.

I got these in the space of about a minute, maybe less than that:

"Strangers become lovers."

"Lovers become strangers."

"The virgin lusts while the satyr rests."

"Authority corrupts compassion."

"Dispersion feeds reversion."

"Community bests disunity."

"Flesh decays when the spirit weeps."

"Life delays what the devil reaps."

"One on one."

"All in all."

"One on one is all in all."

"Error comes home."

"Truth propagates truth."

"Profit seems lost when loss is profit."

"All is lost when all seems gained."

"Beauty contemplates beauty."

"Fear the fearless."

"Tremble before temptation."

"Avoid the idolatrous."

"Abandon the ambitious."

It stopped at that point. I was still scribbling the final two admonitions when Janulski inhaled sibilantly and declared in a loud whisper, "What luck! It's a tutorial. I didn't expect that."

He was obviously thrilled and delighted, barely able to contain himself, which was a sharp contrast to his earlier demeanor. He positively glowed with excitement.

I was aware also of subtle movement about me, although everyone was in place—a change in the vibrational constant, or maybe moving pockets of air with differing density—I don't know. I just sensed *movement* or *motion*—a rustling without actually hearing anything, an atmospheric perturbation without actually seeing anything.

The mediums were perfectly still and relaxed; they could have been sleeping.

I reached for a cigarette then decided against it, put the pen in my mouth, looked at Janulski. He was gazing at Ted, and his exultation had faded to something approaching fear.

I looked at Ted too, and maybe someone watching me at that moment would have said that I shared Janulski's emotional mood. Because something very weird was happening with the medium. The tiny muscles of his face were alternately contracting and relaxing in an entirely uncoordinated way, as though the flesh had become soft clay or baker's dough and some unseen hand was molding it haphazardly—a push here, a pull there, momentary dimpling giving way to grotesque masks and leering caricatures, eyes alternately rolling and shifting.

This went on for some twenty or thirty seconds while the earlier noted atmospheric imbalance seemed to collect itself about him, as though fusing with his own physical aura. Then it all just sort of gradually resolved—settled in, so to speak—and Ted was no longer Ted. The nose was longer, more pointed, the chin more prominent and bearing a deep cleft; the eyes even seemed socketed differently and the brows heavier; cheeks were wider, smoother. Altogether a different personality was controlling that flesh. Matter of fact, Ted had come to look a bit like me. Sparkling eyes crackled at me and looked me up and down. Then that mask smiled, the eyes softened, the lips parted in a merry chuckle and It spoke to me: "Well, well."

I flipped a glance at Janulski and then back to the living mask. "Who do we have here?" I asked, hoping that I was smiling back. I admit to being a bit flustered, here.

It said, "She did a good job with you, I see." Another chuckle. "Knew she would, of course. That's why..." The mask became disarranged momentarily, then settled in again.

I asked, "Should I know you? What is your name?"

"...bad I couldn't have hung around longer. We don't always call our own shots, though, do we? Well, you're a fine-looking young man. Heard some wonderful things about you."

I shivered and asked It, "Can you hear me?"

Rachel replied, in the raspy whispering voice. "I hear. I will relay."

I looked from her to It, then asked It, "Can you give me your name?"

There was a brief pause while It just sat there and gazed at me with a sort of bemused smile. I was reminded of the look on one's face who is waiting for an interpreter to tell him what someone has just said. *This* one apparently had the wrong slant because It chuckled again, the eyes flashed at me, and It said, "No no, she got it all wrong. I never owned a Ford in my life. Believe it was a Studebaker. Or maybe a Buick. I'm not sure."

Another laugh, another flash of those intense eyes, then: "Time's up, they say. Have to go. She's very proud of you. Stay the way you are. Oh, wait—here's another—someone just gave me ... Selma came home today. That's it. Selma came home today."

It departed, caving in and withdrawing into a small dimple just above the eyes.

The flesh of Ted's face rebounded and wobbled a bit, like disturbed Jell-O, then resolved immediately into his normal features. He closed his eyes and again bowed his head while I gaped stupidly with frozen mind and tumbling emotions.

I heard Janulski say, in that soft, sweet voice, "Thank you. Thank you all for coming."

Then the mediums began stirring.

Janulski cried, "How thrilling, Ashton! You were just awhile ago telling me about your parentage. But I must have misunderstood the earlier message! I thought he was your father in a *previous* life!"

I got to my feet and reached him in one quick step, grabbed him by the collar, and put his face to the desk. "You son of a bitch!" I panted.

"What is the *matter* with you?" he howled.

I let him go but had to hold my own hands to keep them

where they belonged. "Some things you just don't play with, pal," I told him. "If I find out you did then we'll discover which one can break the other in two."

The mediums were aghast.

But so was I.

And I had to get back to Annie's private office. I wanted to see if that sucker was wired for sound, too.

CHAPTER
THIRTEEN

To Know, Yet Know Not

Okay, sure, my reaction was both extreme and premature. But I guess the experience really touched one of my sensitive spots and it also rubbed the wrong way against another of my prejudicial concepts.

I never really liked the idea of spirit communication, you see. One of the reasons for that, I'm sure, is that it offends my sense of that which constitutes an orderly universe. I never really gave a lot of weight to the evidence supporting purported recalls of past-life experiences either, probably because I had never really bought the reincarnation idea.

If I'd had to take one or the other, though, I'd probably have taken reincarnation because the theory itself does harmonize so beautifully with natural science and what we know—or think we know—about life on Earth and mankind in general. Reincarnation—metempsychosis, as it is also known—provides the balancing complement to the theory of evolution. Or, as some thinkers would prefer to think of it, evolution validates reincarnation and vice versa.

So, see, I've never really had a coherent belief-system in place inside my head or else I would not have this inconsistency of thought. I say on the one hand that I cannot accept a disorderly universe while on the other hand rejecting ideas that promote orderliness of the phenomenal world. I don't like the idea that we can talk with the dead, yet I have long believed that the personality survives death in some manner or other. Reincarnation theory provides, among other things, a rational explanation of what happens after death. Most re-incarnationists believe, moreover, that there is a waiting period between incarnations while the soul or whatever is preparing for the next life—so this tends to support the whole spiritualistic concept of spirit guides and direct communications between the living and the dead.

I know, see. I have known these things for quite a long time, at least in the intellectual sense. It's my belly that just does not want to go along, and it was my belly that put me at Janulski's throat instead of taking a long, careful look at the experience—and maybe *then* going for his throat. Because even if I fully accepted spirit communications and all that, it is a field tailor-made for charlatans, and their numbers are legion. In fact, there are obviously more charlatans than mystics in spiritualism. So I don't buy just anyone who comes down the pike. In fact I had not bought anyone at that time, even though I'd encountered a few whom I could not readily debunk. Reasonable skepticism should move a guy just so far, though. Mine had moved me too far too fast in the matter of Janulski and his mediums.

But, see—what really moved me was not as much skepticism as the feeling of trespass into a highly sensitive personal area. Trespass, that is, with intent to hoodwink and deceive. Here too, though, my reaction was not consistent with the experience. The whole thing had been conducted in broad daylight and with absolutely no apparent means of introducing theatrical special effects. I saw and heard with my own eyes and ears; I was very positively impressed that it was an authentic experience, *while it was happening*. It was only in afterthought that I felt the need to reject it.

At the bottom line, then, I have had to accept the unhappy conclusion that I reacted the way I did against Janulski because I almost desperately wanted the experience to be a valid one. I had to prove it. So something in my gut—or something in the way I work—fired me up and sent me via rage to prove it in the only way available: by trying and failing to disprove it.

Well, let me tell you, I shook down Annie's private office —where I had the earlier conversation with Janulski—and found no electronics whatever. Just for the record, one of my Pentagon specialties was electronic countermeasures; I know where to look and how to look for electronic eavesdropping devices.

I had already begun to feel a bit sheepish even before the completion of that search. Janulski had followed me from the conference room and was standing just inside the office in a grimly quiet watch of my activities. The three mediums and two other ladies were hovering about just outside. The sweep required only about two minutes. I stepped past Janulski, told him, "Okay, so I'm a jerk," and went out to apologize to the mediums.

They already knew I was a jerk but apparently they did not know what had set me off. Rachel graciously accepted my apology and pointedly told me, "We are merely channels, you know. We provide the machinery on this side, and that's all. We don't even know what has been divulged unless we listen to the tape or read a transcript."

Ted shook my hand and waved off the apology. "People often get upset," he said, dismissing the entire incident.

Hilda merely smiled and walked away.

That left Janulski. He carefully closed the door to Annie's office as he said to me, as though none of it had happened, "We can check the tape if you're foggy on any of the details. But since we got a tutorial this time we have to have a double verification—that is, two independent transcriptions for comparison—before I can even touch that tape. So it will be a few minutes."

We walked outside and sat in the gazebo so I could have a smoke. I asked him, "You put a lot of stock in these tutorials?"

He replied, "Wouldn't we be terribly foolish not to?"

I said, "I guess it would depend on the source."

He said, "Good point. But we feel very secure about that."

I wondered, "What if it's coming from a mother ship in earth orbit?"

He shrugged and said, "It would have to be a very large mother. How many people would you say pass each day from this planet?"

I shrugged, too, and replied, "Look at how far we've come ourselves already with microtechnology. Maybe they could store a whole soul on a chip no bigger than a single human cell. Call it up and play it back anytime they want to, just like we do in a computer."

He said, "You'll go to any length, won't you, to deny that you met your father today."

I sighed and told him, "Looks that way, doesn't it."

He said, "He seemed like a nice man. I can tell you that he has reached a very exalted level over there. I have never seen that particular effect before. I mean, the way he became manifest. We never get more than vocal effects. But he came in visually both times."

"When was the other time?"

"He came in that way last night during a routine contact with my regular guides. Told me that he was taking a special interest in our project during this time of stress and that he would advise me directly from time to time. He also mentioned you, and I had the impression that there had been a father-son thing between you in another incarnation. But really, Ashton, there's no mistaking what he was talking about today. Believe me, it shocked me as much as it did you. But I can understand why you'd—I mean, the way you felt about it and all. That would have been really too bald of me, wouldn't it, if I could have set up something like that. Honestly, I wouldn't know how to do it."

I said, "Guess I wouldn't either. Why couldn't he hear me when I spoke to him?"

"Gosh that *was* strange, wasn't it. Come to think of it, he didn't give me a chance to speak to him last night either."

I suggested, "It was like a television broadcast, wasn't it. You know like these hookups they're beaming from a remote location to a studio."

Janulski thought about that for a moment before replying,

"Well no, because he could see us. He just couldn't hear us."

I said, "So one of the audio links was down. Could we ask Rachel about that? How she did that relay?"

"Rachel didn't do that," he told me. "It was the guide on the other side using Rachel. She knows less about it than we do."

I said, "She doesn't know much, then."

Janulski chuckled soberly. "You're still a bit shocked. When you stop to think about it, you'll realize that we know all we need to know. That's the way this works. It doesn't matter, Ashton, if it's coming from a mother ship or Alpha Centauri or Cleveland. What matters is that we are receiving help from someone a lot smarter than we are. Call it whatever you like. But good heavens, don't disregard it just because you can't figure out how you're getting it."

I replied, "Oh, I'm not going to disregard it." I pulled the notepad out of my pocket and stared at my jottings. "This is a tutorial, eh?"

"Yes. Of course, we have to decipher it."

"Sounds like epigrams. Most of it, anyway."

"The really important teachings come that way. Don't ask why, that's simply the way it's done." He shrugged and showed me a tired smile. "Maybe that's the only way they can get it cleared for transmission."

I smiled back, told him, "Dear old Dad didn't seem to have that problem. He gave me a literal message."

"Selma came home today? That's what you mean?"

"That's the one, yeah."

"We get those from time to time. It's not so literal."

"What does it mean?"

The smile grew tireder. He scratched his face, looked at the ground, and told me, "I don't know who Selma was on earth, Ashton. But you must. It simply means that somebody died."

I knew that, yeah. I knew that.

CHAPTER
FOURTEEN

A Resolving Focus

Selma came home, yes, but it was Clara Boone who had officially died shortly after I dropped her at her home that morning. She'd suffered a severe stroke—apparently the result of "thrombus of the internal carotid artery"—and died minutes after calmly notifying a 911 operator that she was in difficulty. The paramedics found her front door invitingly open and Clara dead on the couch when they arrived. They transported the body to County General for an official DOA enroute to the morgue. A card in her purse pointed authorities toward a local attorney as the person to notify in the event of death but they had not been able to contact him. I gave them my name and number and asked that I be informed as to the ultimate disposition of the body, then I went to Eagle Rock.

Clara's house was locked but there were no police seals so

I defeated the locks and went on inside. It looked pretty much as I had visualized it in there—gracious and tidy but very small, really—about a twelve-by-fifteen living room, tiny dining nook with access to a cement patio, kitchen, a single bedroom, simple bathroom with just room enough for toilet, basin, and tub; laundry porch off the kitchen.

I poked about, not really knowing what I was looking for but hoping to find another tie to Reverend Annie and the Church of Light situation. It was a bit uncomfortable going through Clara's personal things. I'd barely known her, sure, but still there is that feeling of trespass when you're sifting through the pitiful remnants of a life. Buried in a dresser drawer beneath sweet-smelling but very old lingerie was a savings bank passbook showing a balance of less than five thousand dollars. There'd been no deposits during the life span of that passbook—a period of several years—but monthly withdrawals in small amounts. She'd probably lived as simply as possible; there was evidence enough of that all around me.

This was a maiden lady; seventy-five years on the planet and never married. Apparently she left no family whatever. In a moldy and tattered photo album on a bedside table I found a photostat of her birth certificate, a few yellowed mementos of her school days, about forty faded snapshots with illegible captions but obviously taken a very long time ago and showing men with handlebar mustaches and stiffly corseted ladies. Then there were another twenty or so from a later era—thirties, obviously—each showing a dazzlingly beautiful and glamorous Clara in various costumes and usually with a man but never the same one. These looked very much like promotional stills from old movies.

I hit pay dirt at about mid-album. It was into the forties.

Clara was more mature but still alluringly beautiful. Ten full pages of the album were covered front and back with small box-camera type snapshots, each one depicting Clara and the same handsome young man in affectionate poses. I was sure it was Clara in each of these but I would not have tumbled for sure to the guy except for the blown-up eight-by-ten that came at the end of that sequence. It was a beach setting and I could tell by the background that the photo was taken at Malibu and I could even narrow it closer than that. The houses shown behind the subjects were homes at the Malibu Colony. And Clara had told me . . .

But the guy . . .

There was simply no doubt about it. It was the same guy that appeared in the preceding dozens of snapshots.

And that guy was a younger and handsomer but still un-mistakable François Mirabel.

Did I say pay dirt?

My mistake. I should have said bonanza because I was looking, remember, for ties. And because the five pages following that eight-by-ten were filled with pictures of François and another woman whom I did not recognize. And although the earlier photos of François and Clara were obviously all taken at nearly the same time, this series was spread over a number of years. Quite a number of years, because I watched the growth of a child in that series of old pictures. It was a girl child and she joined the couple in those photos as a toddler. The series ended with her at about ten. Another series picked up at that point but carried the mother and child only into the child's midteens. And there was simply no doubt that this was young Reverend Annie.

A bonanza, yeah, with my friend François tied a hell of a lot closer than I would ever have guessed. It occurred to me, in that realization, that the man was probably in very grave danger. Because it seemed that everyone with ties to Annie was dying.

I hit the Century Towers at just a few minutes past five o'clock and found François all alone in his offices. He was having a business conference with Rome and handling the fast Italian patter with no show of difficulty. I helped myself to some water on the rocks and stood at the window looking at nothing, trying to draw the pieces of my brain together for some kind of a coherent picture of this dizzying case.

First of all . . . *what* case?

I had known from that first visit to Church of the Light that I was involved in something and that it had come to me—not vice versa. I had felt the tingle that raises my hackles even before that meeting with David Carver on the night that Milhaul died; the tingle had come from Annie, not from Carver—yet Carver tingled me too in reverse fashion and set me up for the late-night visit by Bruce Janulski and the urgent summons by one of the world's richest men, François Mirabel.

Everyone was pushing a case at me—even Annie, in that first meeting when she told me that we would meet again and that we would fall in love; this immediately after publicly declaring over and over that she had been a target for murder and then privately telling me that she had known in advance that I would save her. Apparently François had contacted me at Annie's behest. A couple of hours later she was telling me to get lost.

François was treating her like a prize investment and insisting that I protect that investment while also hinting that his interest in Annie went a bit deeper than that.

Janulski apparently thought of her as a saint and would murmur no hint of criticism despite the strange circumstances that brought them together in the first place. And the summons brought to me by Janulski originated, he claimed, in another world, and he even brought me greetings and later confrontation with an exalted spirit claiming to be the father I had never known.

Then, shit, there was Clara who killed Carver and exposed me to Selma. Clara, best friend of Maybelle who turns out to be Annie's mother; Clara, who a very long time ago was beautiful and glamorous enough to be in pictures and spent a weekend with someone at the exclusive Malibu Colony and came away with dozens of snapshots but apparently nothing else and obviously went into total eclipse behind Maybelle and Maybelle's daughter—so eclipsed, it seemed, that she remained a maiden all her life but maintained close ties with Maybelle who also seems to have gone into eclipse at some point very long ago; Clara, whose death today was announced from another world by Dear Old Dad to send me back to Eagle Rock and a tattered photo album.

What case? Surely not the same one that sent David Carver to his death and Paul Stewart raging to the D.A. for murder indictments on a string of deaths stretching backward in time for fifteen years or so and Reverend Annie to Sybil Brand Institute for Women. Surely not the same one that brought the suicide of a despondent homosexual youth, or the police shooting death of an ex-con child molester, or the accidental asphyxiation death of Annie's own mother.

Carver had thought of Annie as a black widow—a nasty critter that devours its mates—and now Stewart seemed to share that view and wanted to pin a number of psychic projection murders on her, as well.

Janulski called her a saint and a spiritual force whom the entire physical universe was girding to crush.

Clara—dear Clara—had referred to her as simply "that girl" but in a decidedly critical tone.

François and Annie herself seemed to believe that she was in some sort of real danger other than that posed by the police interest in her—and, I presumed, other than some malevolent counterforce from the resistant universe.

So what was the case I was working?

I did not have the faintest goddamn idea.

I set my water-rocks on the bar, ambled over to Mirabel's desk and disconnected his telephone with Rome still dickering, opened Clara's photo album in front of him and said, "What the hell is this, François?"

He looked at the album for about one second then snapped his eyes at me. "Wherever did you get this?"

I snapped right back at him and said, "No dice. Me first. What is it?"

He sighed, looked back to the album, leafed through a few pages, sighed again. "How insignificantly the years pass by. But I was quite handsome once, no?"

I said, "Look again, pal. And not just at yourself. Look at the world around you. Who do you see?"

"Her name was Maizey," he replied softly. "We were very much in love. But it was not to be."

"The kid, François."

"The chief reason it was not to be," he said. "I could not marry. A wife, in Paris. Catholic, naturally. Maizey wanted a father for her child." He sighed heavily. "So she found one."

I flipped to the next series of snapshots, the ones featuring only mother and child.

"Same kid?" I asked.

He glanced at the album then did a double take, eyes crackling into the revelation suggested there.

"Holy Mother," he whispered.

"Holy child," I corrected him. "So what the hell is this, François?"

He was too stunned to reply. I had finally seen the guy with absolutely nothing to dissimulate.

But there was no joy in that observation. Because my case had just slipped into focus, though through a glass darkly. And it scared hell out of me.

CHAPTER
FIFTEEN

To Dream Like An Angel

François absolutely closed the book on that photo album and refused further comment on that period of his life. He was like a man stunned and bemused, wanting only to be left alone. I did elicit from him the information that Annie would have to spend at least the night in jail; the judge had set over until the next day the question of bail and apparently the attorneys had exhausted every avenue in the attempt to gain her immediate release.

So I began to wonder about the D.A.'s case and how much more was there beyond the meager chain of circumstantial evidence sketched for me by Paul Stewart. It seemed to me that there had to be some hard core of a case to establish some reasonable presumption of guilt if Mirabel's legal clout could not shake her loose.

I tried to impress upon François—without coming right out and saying it—the strong possibility that he himself could be in mortal danger, but he was entirely noncommittal and apparently consumed by his own thoughts so I went away and left him with them. And since I could not get to the lady directly, I decided to go for an indirect approach to the truth about Annie.

It was frenzy time on the L.A. freeway scene so I struck a surface path through the hills via Beverly Glen and chugged over to Van Nuys the hard way. The twenty-mile drive consumed most of an hour—which was okay because I needed the thinking time and did not know for sure just what I hoped to find over there anyway.

I went on past the Church of Light Center and found the neighborhood where Annie began her life with George Farrel, her latest late husband. It was one of those typical Southern California tracts that were built on the GI Bill during the fifties to house the burgeoning postwar population and now kindly referred to by realtors as mature neighborhoods. Nothing pretentious about these homes but by and large they came on roomier lots than those produced by the land booms of the sixties and seventies when developers could not resist the temptation to squeeze a hundred homes onto a plot better fitted to seventy. That whole big valley had been mostly farmlands just a few decades back. Now it was endless bedrooms stretching the city into infinity and perpetuating its sprawl through the natural activities therein.

This particular collection of bedrooms, though—mature for sure—had no doubt largely ceased to figure into the population explosion, the natural activities now chiefly confined to sleeping. I cruised it once slowly just to get the feel then circled back and pulled into the driveway of the Farrel homestead. It was that soft time of the evening when the declining sun is providing more light than heat, when the denizens are cycling down their air conditioners and opening windows and patio doors and beginning to feel neighborly.

One of those was eyeing me openly from the next yard as I stepped out of the Maserati. She had cotton-puff hair and deeply tanned skin, wore faded denim cutoffs and a wrinkled T-shirt with no bra beneath, held a small gardening tool in each hand. About sixty, give or take a few years; a plank-owner, no doubt, in this neighborhood. I noticed a Neighborhood Watch sign in a window, and she was dutifully checking me out.

So I showed her a friendly smile and called over, "Hi, Phyllis."

She took about two steps forward before advising me, "I'm not Phyllis. I'm Helen."

I made an apologetic face and said, "Oh!—right!—Helen!—sorry—but it's been awhile, hasn't it. How've you been?"

I was already walking away which was okay with Helen because she couldn't place me anyway. I shot a glance over the shoulder as I turned the corner of the garage; she had given up already and was attacking a flower bed at the property line. I was in luck because the garage shielded Farrel's front door from Helen's view and that door proved a bit more resistant than Clara's had been. Took me nearly a minute to get inside.

It was uncomfortably warm and close in there with the windows and draperies all closed and the air conditioner turned off. I opened the place up and let in some fresh air then just prowled the rooms and opened myself up to whatever might be waiting there for me.

It was a nice home—expensively furnished and tastefully decorated—three bedrooms and den, two baths, nice modern kitchen that obviously had recently been remodeled and updated, fairly large living room with a dining ell. Had a baby grand piano, large-screen TV and VCR, nice stereo system. Several framed eight-by-ten photos on the piano showed Annie with a kindly looking white-haired man; these were wedding pictures and both appeared very happy about that.

Two of the bedrooms had obviously not been used for anything but overflow storage for quite a while. Beds in each were made up with only a spread over the bare mattress—not even any pillows—and odds and ends of stuff were stacked about in open boxes.

The other bedroom was as obviously Annie's and George's but did not show much more use than the others except that the closet was stuffed with clothing—both men's and women's—and the bed was rather carelessly made and piled with pillows. But that room was speaking to me and the feeling was rather sad.

I shook back a shiver and went on into the master bath. The tub in which George had suffered his fatal fall was glass-enclosed and had handrails built into the wall above it. I stayed in there for about thirty seconds, just getting the feel, then I returned and sat on Annie's bed for maybe a minute and gazed back through the open doorway into the bath, inviting the flow. Nothing flowed so I went to the kitchen and got a drink of water, stared mindlessly out the window onto the backyard for a while until I felt something begin to move me.

I just stood back and let it happen. It moved me to the backdoor and into the yard. A concrete-block wall made it private and someone had once obviously enjoyed working back here. It was showing neglect now but the flower beds had been well planned and artistically planted, woven very nicely among a dozen or so dwarf fruit trees that were now heavily laden with oranges and lemons.

It moved me to one of the dwarf oranges. It knelt me down and dug my fingers into the earth and put a frown on my face at what was encountered there, then it picked an orange and peeled it and popped a section into my mouth. The orange was sweet and juicy though a bit pulpy; I found myself making a mental note to talk to the gardener about the soil as I went back inside and washed my hands at the kitchen sink.

Then I heard music and realized that Ann was playing the piano. I went quietly to the door and listened from a distance so I would not disturb her at play; she was doing "Ebbtide," my favorite, and putting in the special little wave ripples that I loved so with the left hand. God, she was so beautiful and especially at the piano; I stood there for several minutes watching and listening. There was a lump in my throat and an ache in the heart as I turned away and went to the bedroom and undressed. I felt very sad and terribly depressed but I was not sure why. It was time for my bath but I did not want to disturb Ann at play so I went on alone and closed the bathroom door tightly so she would not hear the water and leave the piano.

I got the water adjusted just right and sprinkled in the salts, then went back into the bedroom for another quick listen because I could not hear her with the water running and the door closed. She had moved from "Ebbtide" into "Autumn Leaves" and so beautifully, but "Autumn Leaves" always made me sad so I did not linger but returned quickly to my bath and stepped into the tub.

The damned glass doors—they were great for showering but too damned confining during a comforting soak in the tub. I stood there debating for a moment whether to slide the door closed or leave it open but I began to feel dizzy and wondered if maybe I should just get back out and forget the bath for now.

I turned off the water and heard Ann calling me and I knew that something was terribly wrong. I could not turn around to get out of the tub. Something was terribly wrong and Ann was calling.

Ann . . . God! . . . Ann honey! Everything was black. I was plunging through space. Then something hit my head and the pain was sickening, nauseating. I was losing consciousness. Ann—*dear God—Ann* . . . !

I came out of it sitting on the edge of Annie's bed stark naked. I could hear water running in the bathroom. I struggled to my feet and went in there to turn it off. Just in time, too, because the tub was almost overflowing.

For a confused moment, there, I expected to hear "Autumn Leaves" coming from the living room . . . but of course there was nobody there now to play that piano.

I put on my clothes, closed that house back the way I'd found it, and quickly went away from there.

Maybe I had found no truth about Annie.

But I knew like all the angels in heaven that George Farrel had adored her.

CHAPTER
SIXTEEN

In a Different Light

She was born Ann Marie Mathison. Father Tony was an expert horseman, movie stuntman, and sometimes actor who was killed by one of his stunts during the filming of a western when she was only two months old.

Mother Maybelle was known professionally as Maizey McCall (maiden name) and was respected in the industry as a daring stuntwoman. If you have ever seen a forties-vintage western in which a runaway buckboard or covered wagon driven by a female character flipped over or rolled down an embankment or plunged off a cliff into a river, then you might have seen Maizey at work. She and Tony had been married for twelve years and had given up the idea of having kids until Ann Marie came along.

Maizey lost her taste for stunts when her husband was killed. She decided that her child deserved a mother with a somewhat safer life-style so she worked when she could as a stand-in or extra while also continuing to operate the stables and riding school that she and Tony had established in the foothill community of Azusa several years earlier.

When Ann Marie was three, Maizey got a break with a supporting role in a television series—a western, naturally. She had never thought of herself as an actress but she was still quite beautiful and looked much younger than her forty years, and I guess the role was not too demanding; she still worked primarily with horses. That only lasted a couple of seasons, though, and there ensued a period of several years during which Maizey apparently worked at nothing. She sold the horse ranch in Azusa and moved into a Hollywood apartment with Ann Marie where they lived until her marriage to Wilson Turner, an insurance broker, when Ann Marie was ten.

Turner was a widower and about ten years older than Maizey. Mother and daughter moved to his fashionable home in the Los Feliz section of Hollywood where they lived until Turner died eight years later. It turned out that he had been living beyond his means and was deeply in debt. Even the house was heavily burdened with mortgages that left very little equity. The upshot was that Maizey was left virtually penniless. She and her daughter moved to modest quarters in a rundown section of Hollywood for several months pending Ann's graduation from high school, after which Maizey—now in her fifties—found a live-in job at a boarding stable near San Fernando. Ann Marie married Hollywood High classmate Nathan Sturgis and the newlyweds moved in with his parents.

That marriage was apparently an immediate disaster and ended very quickly. Ann Marie went on with her young life, though, and Maizey seemed content with her own lot for the next few years. But mother and daughter became estranged and were not reconciled until shortly before Maizey's death by asphyxiation at the age of seventy-two.

I get all this history not from Annie or François or the cops but from the screenwriter who was present at Church of the Light on the night Herman Milhaul dramatically took his own life. His name is Arnold Tostermann. He is a handsome and distinguished gentlemen of sixty-eight years and has worked in the industry for more than four decades. Writers get around and they tend to know all the ins and outs and ups and downs of this very interesting community; what is better, they have an innate curiosity and a strong dramatic sense so they are usually alert to the pulse of the business and the personalities that drive it. They are really the very heart of Hollywood. Forget all that ego stuff from the directors; the writers are where it is at—and they are even there before the it. "In the beginning was the word . . ." and it's still like that. It all begins with a script, and from that script the entire industry finds its sustenance—actors, directors, producers, cameramen, set designers, soundmen, makeup artists and costumers, all the technical crafts and even the typists and secretaries, publicity people, accountants, studio executives, agents; everyone who works in this town feeds from the hand of the writer, and they all know it.

But there is something even more special about Arnold

Tostermann. This is the guy who introduced Maizey McCall to young François Mirabel.

It is ten o'clock and the night is unusually balmy so we are seated on the garden patio of Tostermann's hillside home in Laurel Canyon. This house has been here awhile, but then so has Arnold. He bought it for a song in 1950 and has watched the property appreciate "about a thousand percent" but never saw any reason to sell. I doubt that you could pry him out of there with a crowbar. He has the look of a self-satisfied man, a guy who has carried the fire and found it comfortable, and you just sort of know that this sense of satisfaction permeates the personal life, as well.

His wife is at least thirty years younger than he, maybe more—very pretty and shapely, poised, pleasant. Her name is Joan and she carries herself like a dancer. Joan has not joined us on the patio but she is back and forth a lot, very attentive, pushing food and drink at us.

We are bathed in the reflected dancing lights of a Mexican fountain that dominates this garden. The lights are submerged in the pool of the fountain and set to beam vertically onto the tiered bowls and falling streams; there are six of them, each a different color and sequenced to flash on and off in rhythmic patterns of dancing light. So as I look at my host I see him in constantly changing hues and sparkling patterns; the effect is sometimes weird.

"I don't know, Ash—okay to call you Ash?—sometimes I don't know what the future holds for young people in this town. Don't get me wrong; it's a very dynamic industry and the new technologies make it all the more exciting—you know, like subscription TV and the videocassette markets—

all very hungry right now—but it's not the same business I started in forty-odd years ago."

He smiles, sips at his wine, looks to see how I'm doing with mine.

"I don't know, I guess it was just a closer community then. More of a *sense* of community, I guess. I mean the days of Zanuck and Goldwyn and . . . you know. Nowadays a young writer may never even meet a studio head, never mind dining with him."

He chuckles.

"In fact, if he doesn't read the trades every day he probably won't know who's heading the studio at any given moment. We have become conglomerated, taken over by accountants and corporate climbers who measure artistic value nowhere but in the quarterly reports."

Another chuckle.

"What in the world would one of those guys find to discuss over dinner with a writer?"

"François doesn't fall into that category?"

"More and more, now, I guess he does; yes. But with a difference. He came to this town with love and fascination, and I mean he loved every aspect of it. Never met a man with more enthusiasm, more sense of adventure, more delight in tackling something new. He got into all our heads. I mean writers, directors, actors, all of us. He was a charming guy. You know, it's strange for this town but I don't think I know anybody who really dislikes François Mirabel. He's just . . ."

"Know what you mean, yeah."

"Exactly. Even stumbling around with the language the way he does . . . I think it adds to the charm."

I am thinking about dissimulation but I nod my head and agree.

"Of course, between you and me, Ash, he uses that to his own advantage. Like my Mexican gardener. Been coming here once a week for at least the past ten years. Can't understand a damned thing I want to tell him but he has no problem whatever when it comes to a discussion of his monthly bill for services."

I sip the wine and watch sparkling jewels of light play across my host's face and I am thinking about a different Hollywood, a young Hollywood still filled with the excitement of its own magic and the romance of its possibilities as I say to Tostermann, "So it was you more than anyone else who helped François get his feet down and find his way in this town."

I get a surprised blink of the eyes. "Did I say that?"

He did not, but I smile and reply, "Didn't you?"

"Never really thought of it like that but I suppose that could be true." His face is cast in blue now, and the silvery hair sparkles with ruby highlights. "Drove him out to Malibu his first week in town; he bought Sol Hirsch's house the next day. Gorgeous place, cost a bundle. And I introduced him to Ed North and several other top writers. Ed had just done *The Day the Earth Stood Still* for Fox, and François was very impressed by that piece of work. Introduced him to Robert Wise, too, director of that film. Yes uh, guess you could say I helped him find his way around. Didn't take long, though, until the town started coming to *his* door."

"The women too, I take it."

"Well now don't get the idea he was a womanizer because he was not, or at least not openly so. Face it, though—this guy was young, he was handsome and charming, he was

French, and he was filthy rich. I have found that to be a combination guaranteed to discourage lonely nights." He chuckles. "Especially in this town."

"His wife . . . ?"

He gives me a green grimace. "Sickly, I think—or, at least, very delicate health. She wouldn't travel, stuck close to Paris, wouldn't even go to Cannes. So François would be over here for sometimes two or three months running. He did not womanize, let me say that. But he did not have many lonely nights, either, I'd have to say."

"So his relationship with Maizey McCall was . . ."

"Oh, well—no—that changed everything. He was crazy about Maizey, if you'll pardon the poetry. But that's a good way to describe their early relationship . . . pure poetry. They were very much in love. But François was not the kind of man to divorce an ailing wife. And Maizey was not the kind of woman to be kept by a man forever. And she had this kid. So . . . very sad." A ruby smile, then: "But of course I was not writing that script, otherwise the wife would have conveniently died ten years earlier than she did, and I would fade out with the two lovers walking hand in hand into the sunset."

"How would you have handled the kid? In your script, I mean."

"I'd have to find her a royal prince of the line, wouldn't I? Anything less would be anticlimactic for a kid named Mirabel."

"Or make her a movie star," I suggest.

"A very big star, maybe."

"How about television evangelist?"

He shows a rainbow smile to ask, "What?"

"Isn't that what you were doing at Church of the Light? Checking out Reverend Annie for television angles?"

"Oh that. Yes. See what you mean. Wouldn't *that* make a hell of a story."

A glimmer in the eyes is followed by a totally blue grimace. "Jesus H. Christ! No! Annie...? Little Ann Marie...?"

I show him what has to be a dazzlingly red smile as I feed that glimmer. "Want to reconsider that script, Arnold?"

"It appears," he replies musingly, "as though someone already did that."

CHAPTER SEVENTEEN

Hollywood Mystique

The night was wearing on but I was in easy striking distance from the Los Feliz area so I decided to give it a shot. The address I had for the Sturgis family was more than fifteen years old but the telephone directory still carried a listing there; I figured what the hell.

Laurel Canyon dumps off near the western end of Hollywood Boulevard; the Los Feliz neighborhood snuggles into the hills at the southern approaches to Griffith Park, east of downtown Hollywood. It's maybe a ten-minute run across, that time of night. But don't try it on a Saturday. That's cruisin' night; you'll find fifty thousand kids in ten thousand cars solidly gridlocked along Hollywood Boulevard between La Brea and Western with ten thousand blaring radios, just socializing in this modern motorized version of the mating ritual.

Weeknights are different. I had an easy run; almost enjoyed it. Hollywood Boulevard can be enjoyable still. It's not Broadway in Manhattan but you'll see even more colorful scenery sometimes—punk rockers in leather and chains and electric hair, sidewalk vendors, pimps and hipsters, hookers male and female, shopping-cart ladies, winos and beggars, sex shops and porno theaters. All that glitters is not gold or even brass but sometimes it can be fun to just drag the boulevard and be reminded.

This is not the Hollywood of old, no. Not the Hollywood where hopeful stars of the future are discovered at soda fountains, not the Hollywood where Bogey and teenager Bacall rendezvous at the corner of Hollywood and Vine to hold hands and sigh and entertain forbidden dreams—but it's still Hollywood and the mystique still drifts in the atmosphere there. You can catch it if you try.

So I dragged the boulevard all the way to Western then jumped up to the wriggly residential streets above Los Feliz, and I found the place at almost exactly eleven o'clock. Bad time to go calling, even on friends, but I had a hunch that would not let me go and I had to give it a try.

Worked out okay. Wayne Sturgis seemed a very nice man —open, receptive—fifty-five or so, slightly balding, a worn-in smile—dignified but not stuffy, nice looking.

I identified myself at the door and told him right up front what I was about. He glanced back inside then stepped onto the porch with me and pulled the door shut.

"I'd ask you in but I think my wife has gone to bed."

I said, "That's okay."

"Hate to disturb her. She's been having trouble sleeping."

I said, "Sure, it's okay. Hate to bother you at this time of night but it really is important."

"No problem," he assured me. "What can I do for you?"

"Ann Marie is in big trouble," I told him. "The police seem to think she's been killing off her husbands."

He said, "So that's it. A policeman was here the other day. He didn't tell me why. Just wanted my version of Nathan's death—how I felt about it and all."

"How *do* you feel about it?"

"It's been seventeen years. What am I supposed to feel? If you mean do I blame Ann for it, the answer is no, I do not blame anybody for it. Nathan was screwed up, that's all. Not his mother's fault, not my fault. Certainly not Ann's fault. They were both just kids, I mean really *kids*. I thought it was a mistake at the time, but what the hell can you do except give your blessing and hope for the best? Ann woke up in time and got out of it, that's the way I look at it. I'm not even sure if Nathan killed himself over her. He had . . . other problems."

"What other problems?"

Sturgis took my arm and walked me into the yard, obviously to distance the conversation from the house. He said, "We thought of Ann as one of our own. She was in this house every day for two years. She and Nathan were pals. They hung out together, played records, studied, walked down to the malt shop, went to the movies. Understand? They were pals. But I never saw them touching each other. I don't think they'd ever kissed, or even held hands. It worried me, let me tell you."

"What worried you?"

"Didn't seem natural. Know what I mean? Nathan was

never . . . too masculine. This friendship with Ann—that was okay, that was fine, there doesn't always have to be a sexual thing between boys and girls—but there weren't any other girls, see. There weren't any boys either. I mean, you know, he had nothing in common with other males his age."

I put it to him point-blank. "Did you suspect that your son was gay?"

Sturgis placed his hands on his hips and gazed into the sky. "Of course he was gay," he replied softly. "That marriage was never consummated. I went with Ann myself to file for the annulment."

"Did she tell you Nathan was gay?"

"Nawww. She did say they hadn't had sex."

"What did she give as her reason for the change of heart?"

Sturgis tossed a glance at his house, moved me a few feet closer to the street, said, "She told me that she and Nathan married for the wrong reason. They were dear friends but simply not in love. She claimed the marriage was for convenience and she felt guilty about that; she was just using us to solve her own problems and it wasn't fair to Nathan, wasn't fair to us. That was a very grown-up little girl, let me tell you."

"But you still came to the conclusion that Nathan was gay."

"I knew damned well he was gay. The only damned reason I blessed the marriage in the first place was . . ."

I sighed, said, "To prove you were wrong."

He sighed too, glanced again at his house, said, "It's a dumb world, isn't it."

I asked him, "Concerned about Mrs. Sturgis?"

"She's a worrier," he replied. "Frets if the cat doesn't eat, frets if it eats too much—or if it doesn't play or plays too much. Mary likes the world at even keel."

I asked, "She get over Nathan okay?"

"She'll never get over it," he replied softly.

I said, "Yeah. Well . . . I'm sorry to revisit all this on you but . . ."

"No no, I'm glad you came to see me. I've been wondering ever since the cop was here."

"Have you kept in touch with Ann?"

He made a face and replied, "Oh, not directly anymore. For a few years there, we did. It was just that . . . Mary couldn't let it go. Every time Ann called or dropped by, Mary cried all night. I guess Ann knew that. Anyway, the visits stopped and the calls became more infrequent. We haven't heard from her in, oh, fifteen years maybe."

I said, "You knew she'd become a minister."

He said, "Oh yes. Didn't surprise me one bit. Always was a deep kid, very serious about life. I'm just surprised it took her so long to get it together."

I said, "Well it took several marriages to put it together. She had lousy luck with each of them. This cop thinks she's a black widow."

Sturgis coughed into his hand and said, "That's ridiculous! A sweeter girl was never born. That girl was an angel. I'll tell anybody that."

Black widow . . . saint . . . angel. What else?

I asked, "Ever attended one of her services?"

"No, I . . . Ann knows where we live. If she wants contact, she'll make it."

I asked, "Ever get the feeling that she was psychic?"

He replied, "If you mean like woman's intuition, yes; she showed plenty of that. Come to think of it, I used to wonder sometimes if she was reading my mind."

I lit a cigarette and offered him one; he declined. "Were you in love with her, Wayne?" I inquired casually.

He said, "Hey! I told you she was like my own."

I said, "*Like* your own is not quite the same, and it isn't even that unusual if she *were* your own. Quite common, in fact. Not talking incest, of course."

"Well just so we keep that distinction," he said. "I wouldn't have touched her for the world but . . . what the hell, sure, I'm not ashamed to say I was attracted to her that way but we're not dogs, are we?—we're influenced by more than animal instincts. I felt very protective, very . . ."

"She in love with you?"

Sturgis took an agitated step backward, crossed his arms at his chest, said, "What the hell is this?"

I told him, "No offense intended. I am trying to understand."

"What are you trying to understand?" he asked, softening.

"Not counting Nathan," I explained, "Ann Marie has taken three husbands, all considerably older than her. Is she attracted to older men? A father substitution? Or is it something else?"

"How much older than her?" he asked quietly.

"Two of them," I said, "were older than you are right now."

He said, "Yes, that's interesting."

Again I asked, "Was she in love with you, Wayne?"

He said, "It's crazy."

I said, "Did she hang around the house because of Nathan or because of you? Did she marry Nathan as a way of remaining close to you?"

He said, "This is really crazy."

The porch light came on and the door opened. A very

aged lady wearing a bathrobe shuffled into view and called out in a querulously wavering voice, "Wayne? Are you out here?" She spotted us, cried almost angrily, "What in the world are you doing out here in the middle of the night?"

I looked at Wayne and said, "Your mother?"

Wayne looked at me and said, "My wife."

I said, "Would you mind if I asked—?"

"Wayne! You get in here this minute!"

"Guess I'd better—"

"May I ask Mary's maiden name?"

"Boone."

"Boone?" I needed confirmation on that one.

"Yes. Maybe you've heard of her. She was a silent film star."

"Wayne!"

"She have a sister named Clara?"

"Half-sister, yes. They haven't spoken for years. I keep telling her it's going to be too late some day, but—"

"Already too late," I told him. "Clara went home today."

"What?"

"Wayne! Get in here!"

"I'd better be going. Hope I helped."

Maybe he did and maybe he didn't.

But it was really crazy, yeah.

CHAPTER EIGHTEEN

Patterns from the Loom

So . . . are you beginning to see the weave of this tapestry? Or are you already way ahead of me? That's okay. Just don't get too far ahead because the woof is still not all that distinguishable from the warp and it could be very easy at this point to leap to a false conclusion. I was diligently trying to avoid that, to keep an open mind and a balanced perspective.

That can be hard to do when you are immersed in a situation with as many cross-connections as this one. It's like trying to figure out where you're at in a television soap opera if you can't watch it every day. Like, you know Jane got raped by Jim after Jean stabbed John and Jake exposed Jim as John's illegitimate son and therefore Jean's half-brother, which makes Jim's marriage to Jean an incestuous relationship, so now Jane is carrying Jim's child though married to Jake who is really in love with Jean. Maybe we can follow that okay, but if we missed yesterday's episode in which it was revealed that John's second wife, Jill, is really Jason—Jake's brother—after a sex-change operation, and now Jill has the hots for Jim and Jean has the hots for Jill but Jill wants to adopt the baby Jane is carrying by Jim, then maybe we don't fully understand why Jake is so furious about the whole thing.

I was not too far from that state of confusion in trying to follow the threads of this case.

Life is not a soap but both lather up and sometimes you cannot tell the suds apart. Bruce is gay and talks to spirits who send him to me on behalf of Ann but I had found Ann on my own just in time to collect the dying fragments of Herman who is also gay but apparently did not listen to the spirits and wanted to kill Ann who is deeply involved with François whom I have known for years so accepted a commission to protect Ann from some nebulous threat although police authorities feel that Ann *is* the threat after taking note of a web of death around her, including that of her own mother, Maybelle, good friend of Clara who may or may not talk to spirits but certainly expects eternal life and who sent me into the golden past of Hollywood to find my same old friend François as a young romantic married to a sickly recluse and loathe to sleep alone in a foreign land so probably consoled himself briefly with Clara and more enduringly with Maizey who is really Maybelle so spurned illegal encampment with François for the sake of Ann who seven or eight years later fled to Nathan who is gay or maybe to Wayne who is not but considerably older although not nearly as old as his wife Mary who is Clara's sister. Ann settles for neither but goes on to wed and mourn—or wed and devour, depending on the point of view—three older men including George who is Bruce's father, and maybe she now has her cap set for same old friend François and the circle is complete.

Or is it?

If you lay it out in a flow pattern, it goes like this: Ann Marie is born. Father Tony dies. Mother Maybelle, or Maizey, falls in love with François—but Ann Marie is alive and dependent, so the love affair dies. Maybelle marries Wilson Turner for stability but eight years later Wilson dies thoroughly destabilized. Ann Marie shifts her dependency to Nathan, and Nathan dies. She then marries Donald, Larry, and George in successive dependencies, and they each die.

Enter, now, a different pattern. Ann Marie has got it together. Apparently she is dependent on no one—but quite a lot now seems to be dependent on her. So what else is different? The pattern of death is different, and I need to get a better understanding of that.

It was getting onto midnight and it had been a hell of a long day but I could not cut and run home with all this stuff seething in the brainpan so I decided to swing back through the valley for another go at the Light Center. At least I was making my way home; I could take the Ventura Freeway on over to Las Virgenes and go home the back way through Malibu Canyon. This is what I had loosely in the mind anyway when I pulled off the freeway at Van Nuys.

Twenty or more cars were still in the parking lot when I reached the center and there were plenty of lights at work but apparently the late activities there had concluded and the place was emptying. I found a uniformed security cop loitering in the gazebo I'd shared twice that day with Janulski; I introduced myself and invited him for coffee. He looked me over and checked his watch; said, "It closes in ten minutes," referring to the snack shop on the property.

His name was Barney, would you believe, a retired navy lifer earning extra bucks the easy way, midnight to eight, to augment the pension. Guy of about fifty, thick black hair just beginning to gray, neat and trim in the uniform and packing a .45 Colt ACP in a very businesslike way. Thirty years in the military puts a stamp on a guy, an unmistakable trademark that says here's a man with self-discipline and staying power, a guy who can cope and maintain. I've always admired those guys because I was part of that system myself and just barely managed to cope with the five years of mandatory service after Annapolis—and the academy itself was no tea party, either.

I bought the coffee in throwaway cups and we took it with a sack of stale doughnuts back to the gazebo. Barney was not officially on duty for a few minutes so we relaxed and talked navy and swapped a couple of stories. He had been seventeen years a chief gunner's mate and had served on everything from destroyers to battleships. Turned out that he'd also pulled shore duty at the Pentagon during part of the time that I was there so we had a lot in common and he was visibly impressed with my stories about ONI, the Office of Naval Intelligence.

So we were buddies by the time the coffee was gone and he had to start his lock-up inspection. He invited me along, which was what I had in mind anyway.

Barney had not heard that his employer was in jail but of course he knew about the Milhaul tragedy and he knew about the child-fondling incident and Charles Cohan

McSweeney—who, it turns out, had been a fellow employee.

McSweeney had worked for the center as a maintenance engineer and general handyman for about two months before his death. Some of the jobs had to be scheduled so as not to interfere with the center's activities—that is, after midnight —so Barney had been in direct contact with him from time to time.

"Okay guy, I thought," he told me. "Didn't say much, but there really wasn't that much to be said between us anyhow. I wouldn't have thought of him as a weirdo. Just quiet, that's all."

I said, "Well, yeah, bent doesn't mean broken. It's just that his particular bend is usually very damaging to young lives. How'd you feel about Annie turning him in?"

Barney shrugged and replied, "What else could she do? Can't have a guy like that messing around a place like this. And some of these guys, I guess, get real crazy. How 'bout this guy awhile back, tortured all those little kids and chopped 'em up? You never know. But I was really surprised about Charlie. Still can't picture him charging a cop, going after him with a hammer."

"That what he did?"

"Way I got it, yeah. Or so the cop said, after he emptied his revolver into him."

I said, "Witnesses?"

"Not to the shooting, no. Guess they'd gone to his house to make the arrest. But there were witnesses to the other thing. Way I got it, he walks in there stark naked and starts playing with the kids. Can you beat that? In broad daylight. Guy must have flipped out or something."

I said, "He had a record of similar offenses, served a

couple of rehabilitation stretches at Camarillo. Guess there was also something about kiddie porn."

"Yeah, I heard the cops talking about that," Barney said. "That's sick—you know?—that's really sick."

I sighed and said, "Sick enough to kill, I guess. How do you feel about that?"

"What can you do with 'em?" Barney replied. "Send 'em to the moon? I figure, what's more important?"

"What do you mean?"

"To society. What's more important? Sometimes I get the feeling it's falling apart around us. Used to be, we all knew who the enemy was. And we killed the sons of bitches. Now it seems more and more like nobody really knows what's important and what's not important. Well I think I know. Our kids are important. These sicko sons of bitches are not. It's got to the point we can't afford them. When you can't afford something, what do you do with it?"

I said, "Get rid of it?"

He said, "Exactly. These guys are expendable. The kids are not."

I report this conversation with Barney partly because it is pertinent to the case but mainly because something he said there hit a nerve cell in my brain and produced a minor flash in there. I'll tell you more about that later. Right now I have to stay with the flow and tell you about something that produced a major flash.

It happened at the fourth stop along Barney's lock-up check. He was telling me, "This is the door to the sanctuary, rear of the auditorium. Reverend Farrel prepares for her sermons in here. She can come and go, see, without going through the auditorium if she don't want to." Then he showed me a surprised look and said, "Hell, it's unlocked."

He had a hand on his pistol as he warily pushed that door open. Suddenly he made a strangled sound and quickly but quietly backed out of there and pulled the door firmly shut, but not before I could see what he had seen inside that room.

He'd seen Reverend Annie, that's what, and he'd seen *all* of Reverend Annie in a bewitching scene not likely to be forgotten in a long lifetime. It's the sort of thing that etches itself into memory; certainly it is etched in mine, though I had but a glimpse.

A narrow pencil-beam from a small spotlight placed high on the wall was providing the only illumination to that otherwise darkened room. Annie was standing in the spot. She was goldenly naked, a shimmering vision of feminine beauty poised in an attitude of exultant worship with the feet together and stretching upward from the toes almost like a ballerina, back arched gracefully and the chest thrown high, head back as far as it could go and the arms raised and reaching as though she were trying to project herself along that beam of light.

I don't know how to reconcile the emotional reaction to something that is both and at once so erotically beautiful and so stunningly *religious*. I just know that it affected Barney in very much the same way it affected me, with an added bonus for him of horrified embarrassment.

"You told me she was in jail!" he muttered, very upset with me.

"Last I heard, she was," I muttered back. "The lawyers must have finally..."

"God! Did you see her? Did you *see* that?"

I saw it, yeah, but I was not quite as willing to accept the evidence of the sense perceptions. An *extra*sensory quiver, back there, had me working along another thread from the loom.

I left Barney to continue his rounds alone and I beat a path to a pay phone near the gazebo.

And, yeah, the quiver had it right. Ann Marie Farrel was still in jail.

CHAPTER
NINETEEN

Wonderful World of Awe

My friend Paul is in his seventies and has spent the bulk of his life as a Catholic brother working with American Indians on reservations in the West. Paul is a gentle soul but you can tell by the sparkle in his eyes that all of life has been an interesting adventure for him; I suspect that he has done a bit of helling around in his time. I mention Paul because he has many interesting stories to tell about the Indians, and one of those will help to illustrate a certain aspect of this case.

One day on a reservation in Wyoming—this was back in the fifties or sixties—Paul and one of his Indian helpers were on an errand far into an isolated stretch of the reservation. They were bumping along a primitive dirt road in a jeep when over against the mountainside, less than a mile away, they noticed a huge silvery object reflecting the sun and pacing them at an altitude of about 200 feet. Paul describes the object as "big as a house" and he very matter-of-factly refers to it as a flying saucer.

He stopped the jeep to give all his attention to this object. The object stopped also and "just hung there" for maybe a minute while they looked at it and apparently it looked at them. Then the object "started stunting"—wobbling, fluttering, dancing around with abrupt altitude changes of forty to fifty feet at a time.

Paul and the Indian sat and watched that exhibition for another minute or so, then suddenly the object tilted on its axis and swooped across the valley toward them at incredible speed to close about half the distance between them before zooming straight up and disappearing behind some clouds.

Paul looked at the Indian, and the Indian looked at Paul; then the Indian, in characteristic deadpan and flattened voice, said to Paul, "Wonder what is."

That was the total discussion between Paul and his Indian friend regarding the phenomenon. Paul said if the Indian ever mentioned the incident to anyone else, he wasn't aware of it.

I tell the story because "wonder what is" covers a lot of phenomena for the unsophisticated mind. Many of us have a very similar way of disposing of inexplicable experience. But strike that word *unsophisticated* and let's include just about everybody in that coverage. The level of sophistication apparently has little to do with the way we apprehend extraordinary reality, except in an entirely relative sense.

I have another friend who is a physicist at Cal Tech and this guy is really sharp. He is very much at home with quarks and other esoteric particles. If you ever talk to this guy in a serious vein of thought, you get the idea real quick that he lives in a reality quite different from yours and mine. I was in his lab one day when he was doing some beta-decay studies, using state-of-the-art electronics that, among other exotic things, measures time in ten-millionths of a second and builds analogs of atomic nuclei.

My friend was searching for antileptons and trying to track their *evolution*, of all things. There are hypotheses to suggest that all matter in our time-space dimension is composed of nothing but leptons and quarks; that is, they are the basic building blocks of all matter. These are rather imprecise terms, however, since leptons include electrons, muons, electron and muon nutrinos, and their corresponding antiparticles; quarks have been subdivided into four subparticles —up-quarks, down-quarks, strange-quarks, and charmed-quarks—and they carry corresponding antiparticles, too.

Well, this guy was trying to analog—maybe theoretically, I don't know, but he was trying to build a model of the transformative processes of leptons during beta-decay, and he had some damned sophisticated equipment to help in that. While we were standing there watching the computer graphics, a strange little sine wave appeared and began undulating along the entire model for a period of about ten seconds.

My friend had bent down for a closer look, then looked back at me when the thing zoomed away, as though to confirm that more than one pair of eyes had witnessed that, then he bent back to the monitor and muttered, "Wonder what the hell that was."

Wonder what is, yeah. Even this twenty-first-century brain had to insulate itself from the inexplicable. My friend the theoretical physicist went on with his studies as though nothing phenomenal had occurred. To this day he has said absolutely nothing to me about this incident.

So I put it to you directly, now. How many times during your daily routines have you seen something, or heard something, or in some way experienced something that does not seem to conform to your preconceptions of reality—then disposed of it by the magic words: wonder what is?

The American Indians, by the way, did not regard their mentally ill as expendable or disposable. They considered them possessed by special spirits . . . and they revered them.

But my pal Barney had looked at his ex-friend Charlie and muttered to me, "Wonder what is."

As soon as I confirmed my suspicion that Annie was still securely locked away at Sybil Brand, I beat it back to that sanctuary and let myself in through that same door, which Barney had tactfully left as he'd found it—and it was exactly as I'd last seen it, except that the apparition of Annie was nowhere about. This is a rather large room, easily twenty by thirty feet, with the ceiling beginning maybe twenty feet high at the back wall and sloping down to seven or eight feet at the front.

My initial impression, with Annie in the beam, was that the spotlight was affixed to the back wall near the ceiling, but it turned out to be part of a track-lighting system running across the ceiling near the back wall. I found a ladder in a janitor's closet and went up there to check it out. It was an ordinary GE sealed-beam spotlight like any you'd find in a modern lighting system, so that disposed of any faint suspicion that what Barney and I had seen was no more than a holographic projection.

While I had the ladder out, I checked the three other lights on that track and found that each had been turned off at the individual switch at the back of the lamp. That was a curiosity because this room had no windows, so it would surely need ample lighting even by day, and the track system was the only source of light in that room. A single pencil-beam could at no time provide satisfactory lighting for a room so large. I turned them all back on and still there were deep shadows covering more than half the area. I decided that the lighting was for dramatic effect more than anything else. Maybe she liked the symbolism of pure white light piercing the darkness in a beamed effect as a play on the Church of the Light. Or maybe it had an inspirational effect for her. Maybe she always prayed that way.

Certainly there seemed to be no other purpose to this sanctuary. The room was plain of decor and virtually bereft of furniture. A tiny desk and a single cane-bottom chair said it all for six hundred square feet of space. A door in the front wall opened onto the stage of the auditorium. So there was a front door and a back door. There was a bathroom just large enough to hold a toilet and wash basin; no window there, either. And there was the janitor's closet, a narrow enclosure running the length of a side wall. Nothing else was there—not a picture or a tapestry or any other decoration. I inspected every square inch of those walls and tested every ceiling tile; there were no lenses, no microphones, no loudspeakers.

It was your classic mystery-movie sealed room. Nothing in and nothing out except via the two doors; there was not even an air-conditioning duct.

I dragged the ladder around and put the lighting back the way I'd found it. Then I put the ladder away and sat down at the little desk and lit a cigarette. And ipso-presto, Reverend Annie reappeared.

She was in the beam of light, same as before. Unblinking, unmoving, not a sound. But this time she was only about six feet away from me. I had a ringside seat at three-quarter profile. It was spectacular. The male animal part of me was reacting appropriately, totally without shame. The rest of me felt like a peeping Tom but I could not take my eyes away.

I thought, what the hell, it's just an apparition anyway, no need to get uptight. But then the smoke from my cigarette drifted into the beam just above her head . . . and the apparition blinked at that.

So I was already in an *oh shit!* mode when those arms came down to its side and the apparition turned to regard me with a solemn gaze.

And this was too real, too solidly three-dimensional. Those eyes were turning me inside out and the figure in the beam was repositioning arms and legs in a modest attempt at cover.

I had to clear my throat twice before I could force words through it and ask her, "Can you hear me, Ann?"

She replied, "Yes, I hear you," but the voice was faint and seemingly far away.

I said, "Sorry for the intrusion. But I'm on the case and I'm at work."

She said, "Thank you, Ashton. Please help me if you can. I am in a terrible place."

I was replying to that, "I am going to—" when she flat winked out, like someone throwing a switch on a light; one moment she was there, the next she was not.

I was thinking bilocation and astral projection and apportation and wraiths and all the other possibilities, but no explanation—at such a time—is sufficient to quieten the butterflies in the belly or to warm the chills that trickle endlessly along the nervous system.

She had *been* there, damn it, in all her physical glory. I could even smell her perfume and taste it on my tongue.

But do you know what I was thinking, at that very moment? I was remembering our first meeting and what she'd said to me on that occasion—and I was remembering the experience at her home earlier that day.

She had told me that we would meet again—which we did, at François's house that same night—and she had said that we would fall in love—which had not seemed too likely, as of that second meeting.

But it was the memory through George Farrel that was coming in the strongest, the sense of utter adoration—and I realized that this feeling was now as much my own as anyone's.

Wonder what is.

CHAPTER
TWENTY

There You Go

So how do you go home and go to bed after an experience like that? I was not really all that tired, anyhow. Besides, I was beginning to get a feel for this case and I simply could not let it go; so at 1:30 A.M., I gathered all my notes and documents together and took them into an all-night restaurant for a breakfast-table review.

The waitress was cute and appealing but I guess I was the only customer at her station and she wanted to hang out and talk while I was trying to assemble my case. She delivered my coffee with a flourish and said, "There you go." I don't know why everyone in food service delivers it with "there you go." It is one of those expressions that have crept into the language by the backdoor—like "have a nice day"—except that "there you go" does not really mean a damned thing. If they would say, "There; now go," that would mean something, see, and you'd get their drift. But I think what they really mean is, "There; I went and fetched," and I guess maybe you should scratch their ears or their belly as a reward but I have never tried that.

At any rate, I had the coffee—but I still had the waitress too. She glanced at the papers I had scattered about the table and said, "What are you, a workaholic? Good-looking guy like you should be able to find something more interesting to handle at two o'clock in the morning than paperwork."

I put down the Xeroxes of David Carver's file and looked her straight in the eye. "Have any suggestions?"

She was just flirting. She laughed softly and replied, "Well not with me. I'm here 'til seven o'clock."

I made a sorrowing face and said, "See? That's the way my luck has been running lately."

She glanced again at the papers and said, "You're not a cop, are you?"

I said, "Do I look like a cop?"

She studied me for a moment before replying, "No, I guess not." Her glance flicked along the papers again. "So what're you doing?"

I told her, "I play with puzzles."

"Oh."

"Keeps me out of mischief."

"Sounds boring. Surely you could find something better to play with."

I said, "Well, I'm always open to suggestion."

She laughed again; said, "If you're still footloose and fancy-free at seven o'clock, come on back."

I said, "Best offer I've had all week. Thanks."

I went back to my puzzle.

She continued to hang out. Presently she told me, "My name is Sandra."

I smiled but did not look up as I replied, "Yeah, I checked out the nameplate. Mine's Ashton."

She said, "That's an odd name. Kind of sissy, isn't it?"

I lifted my gaze to hers and told her, "Well, see, it was given to me by a woman."

Her laugh that time was a bit uncertain but it sent her away. She was back a minute or so later with my eggs and bacon, delivered again with the inevitable, "There you go."

I asked her, "Want me to scratch your belly?"

She showed me a wicked smile and replied, "Not 'til seven o'clock." She fussed with the table setting and I guess she was looking at the paperwork while she did that because she said, "Oh. Reverend Annie. She's in here a lot."

I toyed with the plate of food and casually replied, "Guess it's in the neighborhood, eh?"

"Yeah. We get a lot of those people in here. Specially on my shift. They sit over there at the big corner booth and gab the night away sometimes. I never heard such junk. I mean, auras and out-of-body travel and all that junk."

I said, "All that Bible junk, eh?"

She said, indignantly, "That junk isn't in the Bible!"

I said to her, "Sure it is. What do you think a halo is? And how do you think Jesus appeared to Paul on the road to Damascus?"

She didn't know what the hell I was talking about, but she said, "Oh well, that was in the old days."

I said, "Right, right. This is the New Age, isn't it."

"Sure. You can't do that stuff anymore. And I'd think they would have something more interesting to do with their time than sit around and talk about that junk."

I said, "Well maybe they like puzzles, too."

Her eyes flashed to my paperwork. She said, "I think they like sissies, too. Are you one of them?"

I chuckled. "One of what?"

"Half of those men are gay. Now don't tell me you're gay, Ashton."

I said, "I didn't tell you that, Sandra. Which men are you talking about?"

"Those guys from Reverend Annie's. Are you part of that bunch?"

I said, "No. But they are my puzzle, you see."

She said, "I think you're part of the puzzle, handsome. Never mind seven o'clock. I've got something interesting to do."

Sandra went away, then, and left me alone after that. I tackled both my food and my puzzle and did not see her again until I was leaving. Another girl brought me a refill of coffee halfway through the meal and uttered not a word.

Sandra took my money at the cashier's stand, deadpanned it as she gave me my change, but she did say, "Have a nice day."

I replied, "There you go," and paused at the door to put the change away.

Sandra called after me, very quietly, "They're fruits and nuts, Ashton. All of them. Better you should find something more natural to play with."

I turned back and said, "Thanks. I'll keep that in mind."

She said, in that same controlled tone, "And that Annie bitch is the fruitiest of them all. I think she's really a man, in drag."

I told her, "You're wrong about that, kid. You are dead wrong about that."

And she told me, "Then she's a butch lesbian. And I am *never* wrong about that."

I hoped she was wrong about that. God, I hoped so.

Maybelle had been dead for more than two months but her house looked undisturbed—probably very much the same as it had been when they carried her away, except that the utilities had been disconnected. I doubted that there had been time to move the estate through probate. With her daughter as executor, that probably was not being pushed. Annie had been a very busy lady, of late. Besides, it can be very traumatic going through all the personal possessions and trying to decide what to keep and what to throw away. Not that there were a lot of those. Maybelle, like Clara, had lived simply.

I used a pencil-flash to find my way around, and tried to keep it quiet. Did not need to attract the attention of curious neighbors and even more curious cops. Technically I was housebreaking. Of course, I did not want to take anything away. Nothing physical, that is.

I did check out the kitchen stove, though. The bedroom where Maybelle had slept was off the kitchen and it was the stove, they say, that killed her. It was one of the old ones. And it had been red-tagged by the gas company as unsafe to operate. There was no gas now so I could not verify the problem.

I went in and sat on the bed for a couple of minutes. It had not even been made up; was probably exactly as it had been when Maybelle died in it. I got nothing there. So I walked about the house for a few minutes, ran my fingertips along the walls and windows, lay down on the living room floor. Nothing.

I went into the attached garage. Maybelle's car was there. A 1952 Dodge Coronet. Paint was faded, upholstery a bit tattered. Key was in the ignition. Battery was still up; there was half a tank of gas.

Something fluttered me while I was sitting in the Dodge, but it went on past and would not return. So I returned to the house, sat on the sofa, lit a cigarette, and called her. Very quietly. "Maybelle. Maizey. Let's talk."

Nothing.

I tried for about five minutes then went to dispose of the cigarette in the toilet.

When I returned to the living room, another presence was there.

I could not see it. But I could feel it.

So I tried again. "Maybelle. Maizey. I am Ashton Ford. I am trying to help Ann Marie. Will you talk to me?"

A moment later an indistinct form appeared near the doorway to the kitchen. It glowed luminously but did not illuminate the darkness between us. When I say "indistinct," I mean that it was no more than a shimmering luminosity, larger in the vertical than in the horizontal but no more of a form than that.

"That you, Maybelle?"

"Hello, Ashton." The voice was in my head and I recognized it but she was working through my own articulation centers; I was aware of phantom movements of my tongue as she spoke. "Maizey cannot come."

It was Selma. Believe me, it was Selma.

"Where is Maizey, Selma?"

"She cannot come."

"She left before you, kid. Why can't she come?"

"She is not . . ."

I felt her struggling for a word. I tried to help, threw my whole damned vocabulary open to her, but still she struggled. I tried vocalizing again.

"I need to talk about Ann Marie."

"We cannot help."

"Why can't you help?"

"Different. It is different."

Her appearance was improving, the shape becoming more like a person. I could see a distinct head now—hair, eyes, and mouth—though like white smoke. Gradually she brought it all out, the entire process consuming most of a minute, after which I could see her clearly but still without firm delineation—not, that is, a three-dimensional body with planes and angles but more like a photographic image projected onto smoke. But she was a young woman, that was clear, and she was probably quite pretty.

I asked her, "Are you Selma or are you Clara?"

"I am forever Selma. I have been Clara."

I tried again. "Ann Marie is in big trouble."

But she was holding firm. "We cannot help."

I was a bit irritated by that. I snapped, "Why the hell can you not help?"

"Different. Not allowed."

"Different how?"

"Not the same. Different."

"Not the same plane?"

"That is close."

"Not the same state?"

"State of being, yes, that is closer. We cannot help that girl, Ashton."

I said, "Well shit."

Something like a fine wave of humor moved through me and I knew it came from her. It was followed instantly by an almost chiding question. "Is it so serious, my dear?"

I replied, "It's serious, yes. Where the hell is Maybelle? It's her kid, after all."

I actually heard her laugh, that time. And she told me, "That girl is nobody's kid. She is . . . different. And her . . . consorts. All different."

I had a sudden intuition, and went with it. "It's a different game."

A brief hesitation, then: "Yes."

"Tell me the name of the game, Selma."

"Forbidden."

"Tell me something. Anything. Give me something."

The apparition was losing itself, losing focus or something, disintegrating.

I repeated, "Anything, damn it!"

Faintly: "Azusa."

"What?"

"Go to Azusa."

So okay.

That was better than nothing at all.

I would go to Azusa. And I would find the name of this goddam game.

But I was talking just to cheer myself up. I knew that it would not be as simple as that. Unless I had lost all my powers of fine discernment, Selma had just given me a tutorial on life after death—or life after life, if you will.

Jesus had spoken of many mansions.

All the great mystics had talked about the many states of being and the necessity to progress through them all before any of us may return to God.

Dismiss it all, if you'd rather. And have a nice day.

I could not.

CHAPTER
TWENTY-ONE

Grains of Smart

In the literature that serves as the real history of our planet, from the oldest to the newest, there is recorded indelibly between the lines the saga of an indomitably persistent impelling force that moves the human story along. It is not enough to try to understand this force by simply naming it with a "there you go," especially if we name only the effect and not the force itself.

Some would attempt to define the mankind theme by invoking a single word: evolution. But that names only one observable effect.

Many wish to label it with religious terms alone, such as God's will, God's plan, God's this and God's that—and though such terms may be comforting at times, they go no further toward a meaningful understanding of the mankind situation than they would toward an understanding of celestial mechanics or nuclear physics.

So let's talk plainly here, pal, even if a lot of people get mad at me for doing so. No matter what the angle of approach, whether via science or religion, most people really try to skirt the issue of who we really are and what the hell we are doing here.

I said plain talk, so here goes. Each and every one of the world's great religions is based on and governed by some really insane ideas. Christianity is an insane religion. So is Judaism, and Hinduism, and Buddhism, Shinto, Islam—all of it. Of course I am talking "insane" from the viewpoint of logic and common sense.

Let's just take Christianity as an example of what I am getting at. God made Adam with cock and balls, Eve with vagina, womb, and ovaries—the two capable of re-creating life in their own kind by use of same equipment, same as the other animals—yet sex is sinful for anything but animals, and we are all born with the burden of Adam and Eve's original transgression. God got disgusted with his experiment along about the time of Noah and decided to wipe the slate clean—he didn't like us very much—but we got a last-minute reprieve via Noah, although there could be some question as to whether maybe Noah was no more than the first ecologist; God needed him to save the other animals from extinction.

But Noah's descendants blew it, too, and made God sorry that he'd saved this particular animal from extinction because we were living pretty much like the others—and I don't get the logic of that, either.

But God tried again, and this time he himself descended onto the planet but he did it in a sneaky way—he came in through a virgin's womb, thus rehabilitating the scandalous Eve (somehow) and wiping away her original sin through an act of nonsexual reproduction. But this was not an automatic, you see; first, all the folks have got to believe that Mary was really a virgin, and then they have got to believe that her baby was God incarnate (unless I misunderstand the idea of "Holy Mary, Mother of God"); *but then* they have also got to *dis*believe long enough to put the poor guy to a torturous death *and then* believe. See, it wouldn't have worked without the Crucifixion. I mean, the poor guy had to suffer. And somehow through the magic of insanity, all of mankind *who confess* to the foul deed shall have life everlasting. It wasn't so foul, you see, unless Jesus was God. I mean, hell, all the roads of the kingdom were lined with other poor guys hanging from crosses, and we hardly ever hear about them. So we have to admit that we murdered God and that we thereby transferred all our shortcomings to him. If you don't believe that then you are not a Christian. And even if you do believe it but don't take satisfaction from it, you're still not a Christian. But if you do believe it, and if you like the idea of murdering your own God through your own damned lack of responsibility for your own deeds, then okay: you're saved; you've got it made; Jesus loves you.

See? This is insane. But it works for a lot of people, so who's to knock it? The worst of it, from this logician's standpoint, is that it all could be entirely true.

But I was talking about the impelling force that moves us through all this. God's will does not work it, for me. It's God's will that the stars are there, sure. That does not tell me what the stars are for, what they're made out of, what they mean to me personally. Someone who uses God's will to explain all the events of human history is just plain damned lazy and really does not want to be bothered with anything but another nice day.

But I will turn that idea back, just the same. If that is the way it works, then I feel this way because it is God's will that I feel this way—so get off my back and go complain to God about it.

Would that it were so simple.

Cancel that; I would not want it so simple. Something stunningly beautiful and wondrous and magical and *meaningful* is going on here with us humans. We are involved in a hell of a game. It does not matter that we do not know the rules of play or the object of the game. That *is* the game, I believe: to learn the rules and to discover the object. But the game has subgames—and maybe those subgames have sub-subgames and so on.

If you are content with the idea that the sixty or seventy years of planetary time that have been allotted to you here are all you are ever going to get—and that you are blotto for the rest of eternity—then that is a game, too, of sorts, and I have to respect your game. Go ahead. Do it. Have a nice day.

Or if you prefer to think that you were born damned but that you have been saved by heavenly magic—that you will rot in the grave after your sixty or seventy years until some moment before the sun explodes when you will rise from the rot and reconstitute it as flesh and blood, then you and Jesus will rule the planet for a thousand years—okay, I respect that game, too. You just might get it, and you just might deserve it.

But if you are not quite sure about your game—if you have not yet found the name of it, or your place in it—then you need to come along with me while I investigate the impelling force that gave birth and life to Ann Marie Mathison. Because, believe me, this one is a hell of a game!

Say, for the purpose of discussion, that you are God. So there you are, Lord God of the entire universe because you built it—and you built it *smart*. You built it smart because you have all the smarts there are, and you don't fool around with dumb shit.

It is so smart that you only had to do it once. You took everything that is now present or potential in all of creation, and you engineered all of that into a tiny capsule—tiny in a relative sense, of course, but it was probably no larger than eight of earth's suns and that is *tiny*, that is almost infinitesimal, in relation to the present universe.

That's no big deal, you may say as you place an apple seed in my hand. Can I see the roots and branches, the trunk and bark and leaves and blossoms, all the sweet delicious fruit itself that an apple tree produces in a lifetime—can I see all that in the apple seed?

But, see, the apple seed itself was present in that original capsule; I could not have seen it in there any more than I can see the tree within the apple seed, but it was there. So were all the stars and all the planets, all the gases and the rocks, the bacteria and the viruses and all the living things; all of space and time forevermore were locked up within that capsule eight suns large—and all the people, too. We were all there as the *potential* and the *promise* of that primeval universe.

So you are God and you have fashioned this fantastically smart capsule. With a finger snap, then, you fertilized that cosmic egg and set it off. My parochial and primitive intelligence sees the event as a big bang—but that is also partly because of my limited point of view; a cosmic big bang to me was a gentle sigh to you, and in that sigh was carried all the smarts that you had built into this production.

Smart, yeah, a really *smart* production. All you had to do was sigh and set it off, then you'd never have to fuck with it again if you didn't want to. The sumbitch is self-propelling and self-regenerating, self-maintaining and self-perpetuating. You built all that shit into the original design. It's going to go on expanding and becoming forever; you built it good, to last, and you have a right to be proud of it.

But now part of the potential of that cosmic egg (and maybe even the reason for it), buried somewhere down there beneath the leptons and quarks, was this idea called *life* and you'd provided all the support systems for that, too. Some stars would have planets, and some planets would stabilize into orbitary patterns that encourage the development of biospheres, and some of those biospheres would encourage the development of (or the release of) smartness—nothing like yours, of course, but primitive smartness anyway maybe good enough to begin a little curiosity and self-conscious examination of this whole process. You are God, of course, and you built it that way so you must have been expecting some such development. I don't know why, but you built it and it is there so it must be what you wanted.

So now here we are some ten to twenty billions of years down the pike, and some of the smartness potential you built into the cosmic egg has taken firm hold aboard the third planet of a rather ordinary star near the edge of a rather ordinary galaxy far from the center of creation. You are God, remember, and you expected this to happen, but it still may give you a little quiver of pride to note that the thing is working the way it was designed to work.

So maybe you're taking a special interest.

These little grains of smartness have gone around and named every damned thing on the planet; they've even named themselves *man* and they have developed cultures and civilizations, sciences and technologies; shit they are *swarming* that biosphere and taking it over completely.

Well . . . you built it. Wasn't that what you wanted? Your will be done, you know. You couldn't possibly be unhappy with them, could you, for fulfilling your design?

So sure, you like these smart grains called *man*. You even intend a personal relationship with them, if they ever get smart enough for that—and of course they will because you will.

So here come three of these grains right now. They've come to court to pay their respects.

The first one falls prostrate about fifty paces out and grovels on his belly the rest of the way like a reptile without legs. Not too becoming, really, of a self-conscious grain of smart but of course you understand that he is just trying to show respect. You can't see his face because he wouldn't dare present it to you; he just grovels in the dust and cries out in a loud voice that you are the One God, the True God, the Only God—I mean, okay, it's boring and it's obvious—but you have to allow it, don't you?

So you ask the guy what he wants. He replies that he just wants to adore you. You ask, you mean all the time? He said, yes, Holiness, allow me to grovel in your shadow and sing your praises; I wish to adore you eternally.

You may think that is not so smart. And it may get a bit

embarrassing to have this guy following you around all over the place singing your praises and adoring you in public, but what the hell? That's what he wants, right?

The second grain of smart comes up and hugs you. He claims a personal relationship with your son, tells you that a place has been prepared for him and he's come to claim it. You ask, where is that? He replies that he's not sure but he knows it must be up here somewhere because he gave up sex and booze for it. You ask, don't you want to sing and adore me? He says, no, he just wants to go hang out with the kid. Well you're not sure which kid he's talking about; but what the hell? That's what he wants, right?

The third grain saunters up with his eyes darting everywhere. He's taking notes with a pad and pencil and he's so busy he doesn't even see you until he's right on top of you. You say hi and he says hi. You say, what do you want? He says, shit I want everything—what've you got? You say, okay, that's what I've got; you can't have it all to yourself but I'll share it with you. He says okay, where is it? You tell him that it is exactly where he's at, no matter where he's at it's always there. Use it and have a nice day. He says, there you go, thanks, and goes back where he was because that's where he is. Well . . . that is what he wants, right?

Let him have it, you say. Let them all have what they want. I mean, you are God; you can afford it. Right? You are the one who started this whole thing and it has nowhere to go except where you aimed it in the beginning. Right? No matter what any of them may want at any given time, that's okay because it's only temporary; eternity is a long time for working things out so all the pieces will come together sooner or later.

It's a smart machine and it knows what it has to do to reach the goal.

You are God and you built it with those three in mind.

But tell me, now. Tell me honestly. Which one of those guys did you respect the most?

CHAPTER
TWENTY-TWO

Echoes on the Wind

Comedians have long enjoyed the names of the communities in the San Gabriel Valley, and they have extracted a lot of mileage from them.

"Do you mind if I go to town, dear?"—"I don't care if you go to Cucamonga, my love."

"No, I didn't say I wanted to lose ya. I said I'd rather be in Azusa."

The tradition lives on, with George Burns in a recent TV commercial where he assures us that the Visa card is accepted worldwide ... even in West Covina.

It's all in fun, of course, with no put-down intended. They just like the ring of the names. All are actually very lovely communities that have moved with the times but still provide a pleasant small-town atmosphere at the fringe of megatropolis L.A.

Azusa is nestled into the foothills of the San Gabriel Mountains just minutes east of Pasadena. Close neighbors are the City of Hope and Santa Anita race track. Nearby also are various recreational and wilderness areas. And it looks like it would be a nice place to live—broad avenues lined with stately palms, quiet residential streets with neat lawns and riotously blooming shrubs and trees—good place to raise kids, I would think. You still see white frame cottages nestled in with newer stucco and brick, these neighborhoods giving way here and there to spanking new condo and townhouse developments, apartment complexes, etc.

The old central business district has sadly gone the way of most small towns in this area today, defeated by the trend toward dispersal and the proliferation of upscale shopping malls and trade centers, reduced now to the low-rent business sector and featuring a lot of antique stores, specialty shops, and empty buildings. But it's still an interesting town and very much alive. It officially bills itself as "the canyon city"—referring to San Gabriel Canyon which cuts through the mountains at that point for access to the wilderness areas, the north slope, and high desert towns like Pearblossom, Littlerock, and Antelope Center. There are Indian signs all through that canyon but apparently nobody knows who put them there or when.

I went crawling in there at three A.M. and found a small motel on Foothill Boulevard. Had to get the guy out of bed to rent me a room. It was clean, adequate. All I wanted was a nap, a shower, and a shave—and that's all I got; I was out of there at eight o'clock, had breakfast in a Winchell's

Donut Shop, then went looking for the real Ann Marie Mathison.

I found a guy at city hall who remembered "the movie cowboy couple" who'd come from Hollywood to open a riding academy in the canyon but he knew very little about them; he sent me to the local historical society and they sent me to the local newspaper office who referred me to their microfilm files at the local library.

Everyone was very cooperative and wanted to be helpful but let's face it, thirty-five years is a long time and Azusa ws not a one-horse town even that long ago. I did find a one-line mention of Ann Marie's birth but that is all I had found after a two-hour search of the old weekly newspapers.

So I took a drive up along the canyon road. The deep gash through those mountains was obviously cut by the San Gabriel River from time out of mind as it carried the seasonal run-off of melting snow from the high elevations. In modern times there had been disastrous floods from that river until the hand of man tamed it and corraled the waters behind monstrous dams. Now the San Gabriel from Morris Dam south is a dry rocky bed. The canyon road skirts high along the western face of the wide gorge and is something of a misnomer if you think of a canyon road as a trail that runs along the bottom of the gorge. What runs along the bottom of that gorge is not fit for travel by man or machine—and once you reach the first dam, which seems to rise several hundred feet above the canyon floor, there is more than a hundred thousand acre-feet of water backed up into several reservoirs; the road runs high above those.

I did not travel beyond that point—several miles above Azusa—but turned around and headed back because there simply was no habitation in that canyon. I had passed a couple of horse properties at the edge of town; possibly one of those could have been the Mathison place.

I had no vibes at all. But Selma had advised me to go to Azusa so I was there and just flailing around. And I guess I got lucky. Because I struck vibes at the first stop.

It sat across the dry riverbed upon a small knoll, a really beautiful spread with plenty of shade trees and white corrals, a dozen or so horses in individual stalls and a gorgeous two-story house behind a white picket fence—but it all looked fairly new so I had no illusions that this could be the place where Tony and Maizey had sought refuge from the vicissitudes of tinseltown. I was flailing, though, so I went on through the gate and up the steps and punched the doorbell. I punched it several times, received no response, decided what the hell, returned to the car and stood there gazing about for a few seconds then leaned in and laid on the horn.

An aged black man shuffled around the corner of the house and laid a disgusted gaze on me; said, testily, "Ain't nobody home here, man. Can't you see?" He wore crisp clean overalls and spit-shined shoes, a napkin at his throat; held a chicken leg in one hand and a biscuit in the other.

I stepped back into the yard and joined him in the shade of an oak; told him, "Sorry to disturb your lunch."

"I ain't buying nothing, man," he said defensively. "Ain't nobody else here that can. So you best just spend your time on down the road there."

This guy must have been eighty. Uncle Remus in the flesh, cottony hair and all, but tall and straight and proud and a very intelligent gleam in the eyes. That is when I got the vibe.

"I'm not selling," I told him. "I'm searching."

"Yeah?"

"Yeah."

"What you after?"

"I'm after Maizey McCall."

He chuckled; said, "Shit," then turned around and walked away.

I followed him to a redwood table in the backyard, sat down, helped myself to a tall glass of iced tea.

He gleamed at me and said, "Just help yo'self."

I said, "Okay," and took a drumstick from a Colonel Sanders box. "Call me Ash," I said, around the drumstick.

He nibbled at his; said, "I'm Ben," then nibbled some more while he told me, "She was somethin' else, that woman. But she been gone the longest time."

I asked, "Where'd she go?"

"I seen her on television once or twice. Oh my, that's been . . ."

I said, "About thirty years ago."

"I guess so. Yes I guess so."

"This her place?"

"Lord no. She done sold that place when she went back to work on television. It ain't been around here for the longest time. They done built some new little houses on that pro-pitty—you come up from town?"

I said, "Yeah."

"Then you come past it. Used to be the T bar M, best damn saddle horses west of El Paso; now it's Canyon Country Estates or some damn thing like that. You come right past it."

"Did you know Tony, too?"

He nibbled the drumstick clean then replied, "He give me the job. I mean right off. He come to town one day, I got the job the next. Best damn saddle horses west of El Paso."

"He knew horses, then."

"The best. Best I ever seen. Not like me. I feed 'em and carry their water. That man tells them saddle horses how to act. Let me tell you, whoo-eee, them damn saddle horses don't give him no sass back. They just do it."

"Too bad he had to die so young."

"Yah-suh, that's a fact, that man was too young to die."

"Especially with the new baby and all."

"That's a fact." He chuckled. "Especially..."

"What?"

"That miracle baby."

"What do you mean, Ben?"

He chuckled again and reached for another drumstick. "Just help yo'self."

I said, "I'm fine, thanks. What about—?"

"These are nice folks here. I got my own apartment. I got my own garage, my own car. Come and go as I please, if'n I don't stay too long. Don't feed no horses, don't carry no water. Don't even shovel no shit."

"What do you do, then?"

"I am *ree*-tired."

"Really!"

"That's a fact. Carried water and shoveled shit for these folks for twenty years. They say that's enough. Now I just reelax and keep an eye on the place when they gone. Like now."

"That's great," I said. "Beats hell out of an old folks home."

"That's a fact."

"Uh, you were telling me about the miracle baby, Ben."

"That's what she done called it, sho."

"Why did she call it that?"

"Well, because they all done said she ain't gonna have no babies, that's why."

"Who all said that?"

"All them fancy doctors. She seen 'em all, I guess. One after the other. After they all get done telling her she ain't gonna have no babies, then she up and has one all by herself with no help from them. So that child was a miracle, she said."

"What did the doctors say about it?"

"Whoo-eee. I guess they faces is red. Old Doc Timkins here, he sho was."

I said, "Is Doc Timkins still around?"

"If he is he must have both feet in the grave. That's a fact. 'Cause I got *one* in, and he always been *old* Doc to me."

I said, "Ben . . . thank you for sharing lunch with me."

"You got enough?"

"I got plenty," I assured him.

And I went away from there convinced that I had, even though it was no more than a word upon the winds of time.

"Different," Selma had told me, of Ann Marie.

How different?

"Miracle," Ben said.

That was different enough for me. But I sure wanted a shot at old Doc Timkins.

CHAPTER
TWENTY-THREE

Shades of Difference

I stopped at the first pay phone and contacted François. He was beside himself with anger and frustration. His legal team was continuing to battle a stone wall in their attempts to have Annie released. Complicating that situation further, the D.A. was now preparing to file additional murder charges. I advised François that I might be onto something and suggested that he simmer down and let due process run its course.

François suggested that I was crazy as hell if I thought that he could relax for a moment with Annie behind bars. He also suggested that maybe I was a bit too relaxed.

I suggested a place where François might go and ended the conversation on that note.

Then I called my own number and told the machine to cough up my messages. There were two: one from Paul Stewart and the other from a female assistant D.A. named Alvarez. The message was the same from both: come in and let's talk.

It was shortly past noon when I made the third call, this one to the county medical association's physician's referral service. I was looking for Timkins, of course, and they had two of them in their registry; one was in Santa Monica and the other in Glendora, a community neighboring Azusa, both in general practice.

So I called Glendora. The woman I talked to there assured me that *her* Dr. Timkins could not possibly have been in practice in Azusa or anywhere else in the early 1950s because he had not been born by that time.

Then the doctor himself came on the line, pleasant and helpful, wondering if maybe I was looking for his grandfather who had practiced medicine in the area for more than forty years before his retirement in 1964.

I said yes, that must be the one, too bad, and when did he die.

Young Dr. Timkins corrected my hasty conclusion, informing me that the old boy was hale and hearty at ninety-one and from every indication would outlive us all.

That revelation sent me into a whole new set of shivers and an interesting interview with Jud Timkins.

He still lives in Azusa, though now in a very lovely private nursing home. He does not see too well and does not always appear to hear what is said to him but he gets around under his own power and the mental faculties seem sharp enough except for occasional lapses. Stacks of medical journals and newsmagazines in his sitting room indicate that he is keeping up with the world about him. We move out to the front lawn with bottles of root beer and sit beneath a giant flowering acacia; the old boy seems delighted to have someone to talk to.

"You've seen a lot of changes in this valley, Jud," I suggest, just to get the conversation flowing.

His voice is firm but he has to ration the breath just a bit if he speaks more than five words in a stream. "Sure have. Born here, you know. Mostly agriculture, back then. Grapes. Citrus. Town wasn't even laid out 'till '87, incorporated in '98. Yes. I've seen changes."

"You're older than the town, then."

He chuckles. "I'm older than God himself."

"You went to medical school in . . .?"

"Right after World War I. Hung out my shingle in '25. Right up here on Azusa Avenue. Stayed in the same office forty years."

"Long time, Jud," I observe admiringly.

"Seems like forty days."

"Really?"

"Yes. 'Cept for the nagging. That was good for forty lifetimes."

I grin. "Expect to have that many?"

He chuckled again. "Why not?"

"Who nagged you?"

"Everybody nagged me. Do this. Get that. Buy more. Doctor less. Retire, retire, retire. Hell, no man should ever retire, especially no professional man. It's a shame to just throw away all that experience. I can still tell more from a look into your eyes than most of these kids today can ever

know with all their damned machines. Of course..."
Chuckle. "... I may not be able to *see* your eyes."

"Does it bother you to be old, Jud?"

"Bothers me to be broken-down. It's undignified to be old. Nothing works like it should. Being very old is like being very young."

"How's that?"

"Nothing works like it should for a baby, either. Can't feed himself. Drools and shits his pants. Can't walk, can't talk—just sits there and grins or sits there and complains. It's the same."

"You seem to be doing okay," I say.

"It comes and goes. One of these days it will just keep on going, and I can't say that I mind the idea."

I take a pull at the root beer. "How do you feel about immortality?"

He smiles and replies, "I'm all for it."

"Seriously."

"Seriously?" Another little smile. "I was a medical doctor forty years, Ford."

"Uh huh."

"I've seen it all. Brains, intestines, every organ, every bone. I've seen it all."

"Uh huh."

"But I never saw a soul."

"I hear the soul is invisible."

"I never saw one."

"Ever see a miracle?"

"Saw those all the time, sure. Patients who had no medical reason to be alive but kept on living anyway. Patients who had died, I mean medically died, but started living again. Sure. Happens all the time. We doctors don't talk a lot about those cases because it makes us a bit less than God and some of us can't take that. But it happens all the time."

I gave him time to catch his breath, then ask, "Remember Maybelle Mathison?"

"Who?"

"Also known as Maizey McCall. Stunt rider in the movies."

"Oh her. Sure. Well, she'd messed herself up. Too many injuries. Those crazy stunts. I don't know why people treat themselves that way. Death wish, maybe. I've often wondered . . ."

"Maizey wanted to have a baby, though."

"Sure she did. They all do, after they've fixed it so there's no way they can."

"What was Maizey's particular problem, Jud?"

Maybe he does not hear that because he just takes a breath and plunges on. "Figures have been about the same for as far back as the record goes. One in six. That's the odds. Census figures from a century ago bear it out. Not a modern phenomenon; probably always been that way from the dawn of time. One in six marriages is childless. That's bad enough odds, wouldn't you say. But then she goes out there and throws herself off moving horses, tumbles down hillsides, all that crazy stuff, then comes to me in tears because she can't make a baby."

"But you helped her."

"No, I couldn't help her. Went through the usual stuff. Called in an OB—did the BBT and the semen check, tried counseling, tried—"

"What is a BBT?"

He is talking and obviously thinking like a doctor, now. "Basal Body Temperature charts. To determine ovulation.

She was okay there, like clockwork. Did a sperm count on her husband, that was okay. Found the trouble with a tubal insufflation. That's where we pump a gas into the uterus and listen to hear it escaping through the Fallopian tubes into the abdominal cavity. If it doesn't move, you know the tubes are blocked. She was totally blocked, both tubes. Inoperable, in those days. We recommended that she adopt and we closed the book on her."

"We?"

"Me and these two obstetricians. *Two* because she wanted a second opinion. But she wanted more opinions than that, I guess. About a dozen more, from what I heard."

"So she did find help."

"Not medical help, no, not possible. We simply did not know enough back then to do the sort of things being done today for infertile women. The first test-tube baby was born in England in about '78."

I sip the root beer and speak around the bottle as I remind him, "She did have a baby, Jud."

"Tell me about it. I delivered it."

I raise my eyebrows and inquire, "Normal delivery?"

"In every respect. Beautiful baby."

"Jud . . . ?"

"Uh-huh?"

"Was Mary a virgin?"

"Mary who?"

"Holy Mary, Mother of God."

"Oh, that Mary." He chuckles, purses his lips, chuckles again. "From the medical standpoint, no, she was not a virgin. Not unless they were using *in vitro* techniques in ancient Israel. Even with *in vitro*, though, there has to be a human father to supply the fertilizing sperm. A virgin could be fertilized *in vitro* then implanted without losing her virginity but I doubt very much they knew how to do that two thousand years ago. Even today it is a very delicate procedure, with more failures than successes."

He is fully a doctor again and the old eyes are sparkling with the intellectual activity. I want to keep that going. "I read somewhere once about spontaneous fertilization using electrical stimuli."

He takes his first sip of root beer, speaks almost absently. "I heard of that, too, but I doubt it has ever been done with humans."

"Why wouldn't Mary the Mother of God have been fertilized that way, though, allowing for supernatural influences?"

I have walked right into it, see. He smiles as he tells me: "Because she had a boy. A spontaneous fertilization would always produce a female offspring. To get a male you need the Y chromosome and women don't carry them. Sperm do, and that's the only thing little boys are made of."

"Maizy had a girl."

"That's right."

"Two X chromosomes."

"That's right. An X-Y pairing will result in a boy. An X-X pairing makes a girl."

"What is the actual effect of tubal blockage?"

"The actual effect." We are doctoring again. "Well . . . an ovum ripens inside the ovary and gets spit out. The Fallopian tube captures it and begins working it toward the uterus. If sperm are present in the tube, fertilization can occur. Bang—you've got an embryro right there in the tube. It continues its journey on into the uterus where it attaches itself to the lining and you've got yourself a successful pregnancy."

"But when the tubes are irreversibly blocked . . ."

"Well now they're using *in vitro* to solve that problem in some cases. That literally means in glass. They remove the mature ovum from the mother and place it in a dish with active sperm. If fertilization occurs, the embryo is implanted in the mother's uterus. Nature has been helped a bit, that's all, but all the rules still apply. An X from the daddy sperm produces a girl. A Y from the daddy makes a boy. What's all this about, Ford?"

I smile and say, "Miracle babies."

He smiles back. "I believe in miracles."

I say, "But not in immortality."

"Didn't say that. Said, I think, I'm in favor of it."

"But you've never seen a soul."

"Quit looking for it, long time ago."

"Why?"

"Waste of time. The human body does not have a soul."

"Sure of that, huh?"

"Uh huh. We don't have souls. Souls have us."

"That makes a difference, doesn't it."

"Damn right it does. Hear the same stuff from brain surgeons, except they're looking for the mind. You can't go into the brain looking for a mind. On the other hand, you cannot go into the mind except through the brain. What does that tell you, Ford?"

I say, "Minds have brains."

He slaps my knee. "Right. And souls have bodies."

I grin and say, "See what you mean, yeah."

"It makes a difference. I never saw a soul because I spent all my time messing with bodies."

"Did Maizey McCall have a miracle baby?"

The ninety-one-year-old retired medical doctor produces a long black cigar from an inside pocket, lights it, and says to me, "Damn right she did."

CHAPTER
TWENTY-FOUR

State of the Art

Biblical peoples were not as unsophisticated as modern sophisticates would have them. They lived in a far simpler time, sure, but these people baked bricks and built homes and temples, they practiced agriculture and animal husbandry, they sailed the open seas and engaged in international commerce.

They knew where babies come from, too.

Maybe they had never seen an ovum or a sperm, but neither have most moderns, at first hand. Certainly the ancients had the cause-and-effect relationship all worked out as regards the role of sex in procreation. Perhaps they did tend to think of the female as soil prepared for planting, but of course many modern men think of women as dirt, too. At any rate, the most ancient biblical scriptures refer to the man's ejaculate as his seed, and they certainly knew that any seed had to find fertile soil if it were to produce anything. But they were a lot smarter than that, even, because they knew all about child-bearing ages and the role of menstrual cycles in the woman.

As far back as Abraham, at least, they knew that.

Genesis 18:11 makes that very clear: "Now Abraham and Sarah were old, advanced in age; it had ceased to be with Sarah after the manner of women." That meant she'd gone through menopause. Sarah knew what that meant because she laughed when the Lord promised her and Abraham a baby, when she was ninety and Abraham a hundred years old.

See? Even in that antiquity it was enough to laugh at God himself over such a thing. Surely he jested! But he did not jest, if you believe the Bible. This is prelude to the birth of Isaac.

Can we take this stuff literally? I mean, okay, *faith* has been defined as a belief in something that the senses refute —but many modern Christians apparently try to hedge their faith by rationalizing. Like: "Well, it was never intended that we take this literally."

Baloney.

Those old guys told it like it was. If we don't want to believe it, okay, let's just not believe it. But for crying out loud let's not make idiots out of those people just so they won't offend our twentieth-century sensibilities. Liars, maybe; okay—but not idiots.

When father Abraham tells us that the Lord appeared to him by the oaks of Mamre—along with a couple of angels, I guess—and that he entertained them and fed them—what are we to make of that if we can't take him literally?

What would be nonliteral?

That he dreamed it? Or that he was suffering a delusion? Or that three Bedouins conned him out of a free meal? These same guys went on to wipe out Sodom and Gomorrah. Did Abraham's delusion do that? And was Sarah so deluded, also, that at the age of ninety she hallucinated a pregnancy that produced Isaac, later the father of Esau and Jacob? How much can we nonliteralize this stuff?

The apologists tell us that they reckoned time differently in those days. Obviously Adam could not have lived eight hundred years. And Sarah could not have conceived a child at the age of ninety. No matter how you reckon the time, though, the nonliteralists cannot wipe out Sarah's amusement at God's promise or the entirely literal and common-sense statement that "it had ceased to be with Sarah after the manner of women."

I have to go with the religious conservatives in the matter. Either believe it or don't; but don't try to rewrite the script for your own comfort.

I believe that when one of the ancients talked about sitting down and breaking bread with the Lord, that is precisely what he meant to say. He is walking along a dusty road. Nobody is anywhere around. Suddenly the Lord appears from nowhere and makes personal contact. Often angels also appear: these do not have wings and they are not wraiths; they are flesh and blood and can easily be mistaken for ordinary folks. Apparently they are capable of being harmed, too, just like ordinary folks, because sometimes the reporter protects them from other ordinary folks. Like at Sodom, when Lot took in the same group who approached Abraham at Mamre. (Genesis 19.)

Lately a new generation of literalists have been having great fun reinterpreting scripture from a UFO viewpoint. Also many clerics privately (and a few publicly) have taken to reexamining the Bible in this light—and it does make for fascinating reading. They note that references to the Lord in these accounts often sound as though the reporter is describing a force rather than an entity, and the angels do sound an awful lot like beings who have emerged from a UFO. Indeed, the word *angel* is derived from the Greek *angelos* which means messenger.

Think about it, and remember that these were very worldly men, responsible men, tribal leaders and so forth. They were sophisticated at a certain level, but remember that this was before the machine age on earth. There were no machines. How does a guy describe a mind-blowing machine if he has never seen even a refrigerator or a washer?

Check out this description, from Ezekiel: "As I looked, behold, a stormy wind came out of the north, and a great cloud, with brightness round about it, and fire flashing forth continually, and in the midst of the fire, as it were gleaming bronze."

Ezekiel was a priest, a learned man. In those days, the priesthood represented an educated elite. These guys were like professors of today. Yet Ezekiel for all his sophistication had no model to fall back on in trying to describe what he saw. How would a North American Indian witch doctor who'd never been exposed to civilized technology—not even a pickup truck or a jeep—describe a phantom jet thundering through the skies?

"And from the midst of it came the likeness of four living

creatures. And this was their appearance: they had the form of men, but each had four faces [designs?], and each of them had four wings. Their legs were straight, and the soles of their feet were like the sole of a calf's foot; and they sparkled like burnished bronze."

From the midst of the fire? These "living creatures" seem to be an attempt to convert something technological into something natural (or supernatural), the only way Ezekiel had to relate the phenomenon.

". . . and their wings were spread out above; each creature had two wings, each of which touched the wing of another, while two covered their bodies. And each went straight forward; wherever the spirit would go, they went, without turning as they went."

He's talking about components of the whole, I think. "The spirit" is the whole. Try to describe a helicopter to someone who has never seen or heard of one.

"In the midst of the living creatures there was something that looked like burning coals of fire, like torches moving to and fro among the living creatures; and the fire was bright, and out of the fire went forth lightning. And the living creatures darted to and fro, like a flash of lightning."

Try describing beacons and whirling lights to someone who has never heard of electricity.

"Now as I looked at the living creatures, I saw a wheel upon the earth beside the living creatures, one for each of the four of them. As for the appearance of the wheels and their construction: their appearance was like the gleaming of a chrysolite [a gemstone]; and the four had the same likeness, their construction being as it were a wheel within a wheel."

Or like a turbine?

"When they went, they went in any of their four directions without turning as they went. The four wheels had rims and they had spokes; and their rims were full of eyes round about. And when the living creatures went, the wheels went beside them; and when the living creatures rose from the earth, the wheels rose. Wherever the spirit would go, they went, and the wheels rose along with them; for the spirit of the living creatures was in the wheels."

Without turning as they went, eh?

"Over the heads of the living creatures there was the likeness of a firmament [blue sky], shining like crystal, spread out about their heads."

Okay. Tell the kid about glass domes before he's ever seen a window pane.

"And under the firmament their wings were stretched out straight, one toward another; and each creature had two wings covering its body. And when they went, I heard the sound of their wings like the sound of many waters, like the thunder of the Almighty, a sound of tumult like the sound of a host; when they stood still, they let down their wings."

Ever been in a football stadium with the home team in a goal line stand, fourth and inches? Talk about tumult and "the sound of a host"...

Ezekiel the priest, the son of Buzi, has just described to you his "visions of God" in the land of the Chaldeans by the river Chebar... "and the hand of the Lord was upon him there."

Shall we take him literally?

Why not. Ezekiel was not the first or only biblical figure to describe the Lord in such terms.

In Exodus 13, when Moses and the Israelites were withdrawing from Egypt, it is written: "And the Lord went before them by day in a pillar of cloud to lead them along the way, and by night in a pillar of fire to give them light, that they might travel by day and by night; the pillar of cloud by day and the pillar of fire by night did not depart from before the people."

Later, in the wilderness, Exodus 19: "On the morning of the third day there were thunders and lightnings, and a thick cloud upon the mountain, and a very loud trumpet blast, so that all the people who were in the camp trembled. Then Moses brought the people out of the camp to meet God; and they took their stand at the foot of the mountain. And Mount Sinai was wrapped in smoke, because the Lord descended upon it in fire; and the smoke of it went up like the smoke of a kiln, and the whole mountain quaked greatly. And as the sound of the trumpet grew louder and louder, Moses spoke, and God answered him in thunder. And the Lord came down upon Mount Sinai, to the top of the mountain; and the Lord called Moses to the top of the mountain, and Moses went up. And the Lord said to Moses, "Go down and warn the people, lest they break through to the Lord to gaze and many of them perish."

Moses spent a lot of time going up and down Mount Sinai, which would seem very time-consuming except for an earlier clue in Exodus 19:3: "And Moses went up to God, and the Lord called him out of the mountain, saying, 'Thus you shall say to the house of Jacob, and tell the people of Israel: you have seen what I did to the Egyptians, and how I bore you on eagles' wings and brought you to myself' . . ."

So how literal can you get? These guys were not talking about dreams or wraiths or apparitions. They were describing real-world events in space and time, in the only words available to them. The Lord was usually described as a mind-boggling force, rather than as an individual, and there were always angels around for the personal interchanges.

Thus, in Genesis 18: "And the Lord appeared to him [Abraham] by the oaks of Mamre, as he sat at the door of his tent in the heat of the day."

Very real world. Picture old Abraham sitting there, trying to get a little respite from the heat, when this thing appears from nowhere.

"He lifted up his eyes and looked, and behold, three men stood in front of him."

Three *men*. Where the hell did they come from? And where is the Lord at this moment?

"When he saw them, he ran from the tent door to meet them, and bowed himself to the earth, and said, 'My lord, if I have found favor in your sight, do not pass by your servant. Let a little water be brought, and wash your feet, and rest yourselves under the tree, while I fetch a morsel of bread, that you may refresh yourselves, and after that you may pass on—since you have come to your servant.'"

Ghosts don't need food and drink, do they. And why would father Abraham grovel before these guys that way unless he'd recognized them as angels from the Lord—or whatever you prefer to call their vehicle. Never mind; in the ensuing conversation, it is obvious that Abraham has revised his identification; there are now "the Lord" and "two men."

"They said to him, 'Where is Sarah your wife?' And he said, 'She is in the tent.' *He* said [my italics], 'I will surely return to you in the spring, and Sarah your wife shall have a son.' And Sarah was listening at the tent door behind him. Now Abraham and Sarah were old, advanced in age; it had ceased to be with Sarah after the manner of women. So Sarah laughed to herself, saying, 'After I have grown old, and my husband is old, shall I have pleasure?' The Lord said to Abraham, 'Why did Sarah laugh, and say, 'Shall I indeed bear a child, now that I am old?' Is anything too hard for the Lord? At the appointed time I will return to you, in the spring, and Sarah shall have a son.' But Sarah denied, saying, 'I did not laugh'; for she was afraid. He said, 'No, but you did laugh.'"

The Lord sounds charmingly human there, doesn't he.

The angel Gabriel does, too, in Luke, and advanced years is still no bar to fertility: "In the days of Herod, king of Judea, there was a priest named Zechariah, of the division of Abijah; and he had a wife of the daughters of Aaron, and her name was Elizabeth. And they were both righteous before God, walking in all the commandments and ordinances of the Lord blameless. But they had no child, because Elizabeth was barren, and both were advanced in years.

"Now while he was serving as priest before God when his division was on duty, according to the custom of the priesthood, it fell to him by lot to enter the temple of the Lord and burn incense. And the whole multitude of the people were praying outside at the hour of incense. And there appeared to him an angel of the Lord standing on the right side of the altar of incense. And Zechariah was troubled when he saw him, and fear fell upon him. But the angel said to him, 'Do not be afraid, Zechariah, for your prayer is heard, and your wife Elizabeth will bear you a son, and you shall call his name John.'

"And Zechariah said to the angel, 'How shall I know this? For I am an old man, and my wife is advanced in years.'

"And the angel answered him, 'I am Gabriel, who stand in the presence of God; and I was sent to speak to you, and to bring you this good news.'"

Gabriel is going to be a busy angel, though. In the sixth month of Elizabeth's pregnancy, he is dispatched by God to a city of Galilee named Nazareth, "... to a virgin bethrothed to a man whose name was Joseph, of the house of David; and the virgin's name was Mary. And he came to her and said, 'Hail, O favored one, the Lord is with you!'

"But she was greatly troubled at the saying, and considered in her mind what sort of greeting this might be. And the angel said to her, 'Do not be afraid, Mary, for you have found favor with God. And behold, you will conceive in your womb and bear a son, and you shall call his name Jesus.'"

According to scripture, this is how we got John the Baptist and Jesus the Christ ... and the real world has not been the same since.

Was Mary really a virgin?

Why not.

The first test-tube baby to arrive via *our* medical science did not appear until 1978. But it sounds like our angels have been using the technique for a very long time. And I would imagine that their methods, even way back when, would make our present state of the art seem primitive indeed.

Did Maizey McCall have a miracle baby?

Why not.

I believe what we are calling it now, present state of the art, is surrogate motherhood. And not miraculous at all.

CHAPTER
TWENTY-FIVE

A Trail of Debris

Susan Alvarez was flat too pretty to be an assistant D.A. Soft and bouncy raven hair framed a flawless oval face and luminous eyes, tempting lips, a sometimes teasing smile. With all that, a very sharp mind. She shook my hand and escorted me into her office, sat me down, and went straight for the jugular.

She asked me, in a soft melodious voice, "What exactly does a psychic consultant do, Mr. Ford?"

I decided without even having to ponder it that I would be entirely up-front with this young lady; no games, no cutesy. So I replied, very soberly, "Depends on the case. If it's a missing person, I can sometimes pick up a trail if I can visit the last known whereabouts of the subject. Or if it's—"

"What do you mean by 'pick up a trail'? What kind of trail?"

I thought about that for a moment, then asked her, "Know how a bloodhound works?"

She thought about my question for a moment before replying, "I'm not sure. Why don't you tell me."

So I told her, in my own inimitable style. "Everything that is, smells. Even atoms smell. I smell. You smell. Each in our own unique way. Has to do with body chemistry. Has also to do with vibrational characteristics. An odor is a vibration. The animal brain possesses certain receptors that are stimulated by that particular kind of vibration. When those receptors are stimulated, the brain perceives odor. Okay, so far?"

She smiled faintly and said, "Fascinating. Please continue.

"Certain animal brains have developed particular sensitivity to those vibrations. Some animals are more sensitive to odors than to any other sense perception. A bloodhound is particularly sensitive and has highly discriminating odor receptors."

I was finished there, but she said, "Yes?"

So I took it all the way. "What a bloodhound follows is not an odor that lingers in the air, like perfume left behind in a room by a woman. If you've ever watched them work, the hounds are working the ground, not the air. They are following a *trail* along the earth. It is a trail of debris. If they were tracking you, it would be a trail of your debris."

"What do you mean?"

"All of us are shedding matter constantly. Dead cells, bacteria. Falls off of us in a fine cloud, all the time. And as we move, it leaves a trail. That's what the hounds follow."

She shivered and said, "Ask a simple question . . ."

I frowned and asked, "What was the question?"

"I asked what you do."

"Okay. I used the hounds as an example of olfactory sensitivity. But some brains, including some human brains, have a sensitivity to certain other vibrational characteristics that does not involve sensory receptors. Nobody in science has yet been able to explain exactly how this peculiar sensitivity works—or where the vibrations come from—but no serious scholar disputes the fact that it does work. And that is how I work."

She smiled and said, "So you sort of stand around and sniff the air."

"In a manner of speaking, yes. But not with the nose. You might say that I follow a trail of mental debris."

She said, "Uh *huh*. Okay. Thank you. How's your batting average?"

I said, "Surely Paul Stewart has briefed you on that."

She colored slightly, twirled a pencil to cover it, quietly replied, "The final results are impressive, yes. But I was wondering how many dead ends you abandon before—uh before . . ."

I helped her. "Before the processes of elimination finally give me a score, eh?"

She colored even more. "Something like that, yes."

I told her, "I am not a detective."

She told me, "I know that."

I said, "I was trained for intelligence work by the navy. And I worked five years at the Pentagon analyzing and synthesizing mountains of data that poured in constantly from around the world. I am also a cryptographer. So I have worked with puzzles in a formal sense. I still do that, but less formally. My psychic extention does not provide me with data."

"What does it provide?"

"Call it intuition. Or whatever you prefer. I think of it as a leap of the mind. This is what I depend upon most frequently when I am formally consulting. Maybe you'd prefer to think of it as a different way of manipulating data."

She said, rather curtly, "I prefer to not think about it at all."

I shrugged and said, "Hey, it's your nickel. You asked."

She said drily, "Yes, I did, didn't I. But you did not really answer me, did you. I asked about your batting average."

"I thought I was telling you about that."

"No, what you told me was a lot of double-talk about naval intelligence and data manipulation."

Well, what the hell. So much for forthrightness and friendliness. She couldn't appreciate that. I stared at her for a moment, then told her, "You really want to know if I am psychic. If I read minds and tell fortunes and all that good stuff. Right?"

She smiled without much humor and replied, "Right."

I said, "Okay, but just remember that it's your nickel. It's also your debris that keeps butting in between us. But it's okay. He's going to call and ask you to dinner. Any minute now."

Those dark eyes flashed and she said, "What?"

"Let's refine that. Any second now."

Her telephone rang before she could respond to me. She looked at the phone and looked at me. I smiled thinly and nodded at the phone. She picked it up on the fourth ring and spoke into it: "Alvarez . . . yes . . . uh huh . . . well let me get back to you. Ten minutes. Okay?"

She hung it up, said to me, "What were we . . .?"

I said, "You know damned well what we were . . ."

She said, "Lucky guess."

I said, "Okay. But wear the ruby earrings. He really likes those."

She turned beet red; said, "Now wait a minute."

I said, "Your nickel, remember. As an after-dinner treat, put on that little lacey thingamabob you picked up at Frederick's last week. He really digs that. And then—"

She leapt to her feet; commanded, "That will be enough of that!"

I relaxed in my chair, reached for a cigarette, said to her, "You demanded it, kid. Now, what do you say let's talk about this ridiculous case you're pushing against Ann Farrel."

But that was the end of our interview. The D.A.'s pet prosecutor did not wish to discuss another damned thing with me.

I advised Stewart: "You're spurring a dead horse here, Paul. Annie hasn't killed anyone and she has not conspired to kill anyone. Maybe some others have, but not this side of the veil. I suspect that a masters' game is being played here, but you can't indict—"

"What kind of game?"

"Okay, maybe a very limited masters' but still the same. Like World War II and the cold war and—"

"Like what?"

"Like that but on a smaller scale."

"What the *hell* are you talking about?"

"All the world's a stage, like Shakespeare said; that's what I'm talking about. When things start getting a bit dull, or a bit too distorted, they send the masters onto the stage to liven it up a bit. So—"

"World War II was not a play. It was—"

"It was hell on wings, I know, but look at how it moved the world. The technological advances—my God, the advance of conscience and consciousness—the awareness that brought on the Aquarian Age—it all started there with Hitler and his court of freaks versus Churchill and Roosevelt and their angels—and God what a stage! At no time in history had there been so many masters in the game. Just count 'em, masters on both sides, guys like—"

"Masters of what?"

"Of the *game*, dammit. Look at them all lined up there. Shit, there was Hitler, Goering, Goebbels, Hess versus Churchill, Roosevelt, Stalin, and de Gaulle. That was just the top line. Then you had—"

"You forgot Mussolini and Tojo," Stewart said drily.

"No, Mussolini versus Selassie was a subgame. It contributed, yeah, and there were other submasters operating in the Pacific, but the real top line was the Hitler complex. Hiroshima and Nagasaki were subgame events that stole the whole show, from *our* point of view, but the real game was played in Europe—and if Hitler had found time to get his nuclear program on target, look out. It would have been balls and all over Europe, and probably no more Europe. But I think a balancing factor stepped in, there, and tipped the game toward the Pacific. See, there was—"

"Ford!"

"Yeah?"

"What the hell are you doing? I don't give a shit about your occult theories about World War II. I want to know—"

"You want to know without listening, don't you. Sorry, pal, doesn't work that way. You asked for my sensing. Okay, I'm giving it the only way I know how. If you ask me to teach celestial mechanics to an aborigine, I'm first going to have to convince him that the stars are not just nightlights strung out for his convenience by a thoughtful deity, aren't I."

"You calling me an aborigine?"

"That's exactly what you are. That cop mentality of yours cannot begin to stretch off the surface of this planet, can it. If you can't drink it, drive it, or screw it, it doesn't exist for you, does it?"

"Watch it."

"You watch it. I'm tired of being called in here for consultation and then ridiculed because you fucking people can't pull your heads out of each other's asses. Do you want my sensing or don't you."

"Keep your fucking sensing, asshole. I don't need it. I asked you just as a courtesy. I've got this thing nailed tight."

"Sure you have. But the nails have been driven into your own coffin. They'll laugh you out of the fucking city with a fucking case like this one. You'll have to go play subcop in Pomona or Chino, maybe even West Covina. And even those guys out there will laugh you all the way to Death Valley."

"We'll see who laughs last, asshole. These victims were all tied so close together that—"

"That what?"

"Fuck you. I'm not playing your silly games."

"You don't even know *how* to play my games, pal. Those

close together ties you're so hot about were forged in another world, on another stage. You don't even know where it's at. You'd probably hang a conspiracy rap on Judas Iscariot, wouldn't you?"

"Judas who?"

"The apostle who betrayed Jesus."

"Am I supposed to laugh, or what?"

"Sure, you may as well laugh. You'd never understand that game, anyway. Couldn't have worked without Judas. Very important role. And what about Pilate? They *had* to have *him*. What was the crime? What had the poor guy actually done? How did they make a *case* on that guy?"

"Get out of here, asshole. I got no time for loonies."

"That's what you're doing to Annie, you know. It's the same game on a slightly different stage. Could even be the same masters at work."

"Get out of here, Ford!"

"Or maybe from Joan of Arc! There you go! Could be. Yeah. Could be

"Could be what?" he asked, interested despite himself.

"Maybe you have a starring role and don't even know it. Ever think of yourself as a master gamesman, Paul? Ever glance into the mirror when you get up for the bathroom at night and see odd little lights radiating from your head? Ever see that?"

He was all cooled off, now—almost contrite. And very sober. "You mean like just for a flash, for a second?"

"Uh huh."

"Yeah. It's a trick of the eyes, right?—trying to adjust?"

I said, also very soberly, "No, it's your aura. What colors have you noticed?"

"Oh well...shit, I don't know. Reds and yellows, I guess. Mostly that. Mean anything?"

"Depends," I told him. "Is this before sex or after?"

"Shit, I don't..." He laughed suddenly, said, "You're pulling my leg."

I really had not been pulling his leg entirely, not all the way, but I laughed with him and said, "I didn't mean that shit about cop mentality. Actually I have a lot of respect for the police mind."

He said, "Yeah. I didn't mean mine, either. But I still want your ass out of here."

So I took it out of there.

Took something else, too.

I had known that he'd called me in just so he could pick my brains. And I knew that he would give me nothing in return; not, that is, willingly. My task was to goad him into consciously guarding it. So I could collect the debris.

I collected some, yeah.

The case against Annie, I learned, was not all that ridiculous. The lady was in very real trouble.

CHAPTER
TWENTY-SIX

Double Cipher

There was a direct connection between Herman Milhaul, the hopeful transsexual, and Charles Cohan McSweeney, pedophile.

This connection, as well as the individuals themselves, seemed to be directly related to Ann Farrel and her Church of the Light.

At the time of his death, while resisting arrest for alleged misconduct at the center, a kiddie porn case was pending against McSweeney—had been for about a year.

This case involved several reels of 16mm film that had been viewed by vice squad officers at a film lab in Hollywood.

McSweeney was not only the owner of that film; he was also depicted in it, but as a much younger man.

The hard evidence—the film itself—had mysteriously disappeared before the officers could seize it, which explains the long delay in bringing formal charges against McSweeney.

Herman Milhaul had been an employee of the film lab.

He was also—get this—he was Clara Boone's nephew and a member of her past-lives study group.

Get this, too: McSweeney was a first cousin of Tony Mathison, Ann's late father. So that makes Ann and McSweeney—what?—second cousins?

But don't hold your breath over family ties. There are many of them here and I don't have them all sorted out at this point. I can tell you this much, though. Milhaul was also related in some way to McSweeney; also to—get this, now—also directly related to Wayne Sturgis, who—you may recall—is now married to Clara's half-sister Mary who already had blood ties to Milhaul. So, in some kinky way that I do not understand at this point, Ann was related to Milhaul.

Suds, yeah. Jim is John's illegitimate son but Jill is really Jake's ex-brother, Jason.

It gets worse than that, though

I have this picture in my head. It could be a snapshot but more than likely is a frame from that 16mm film. In the picture, a man and a little girl of five or six are playing together. The man is in his late twenties, maybe early thirties, but I know that this is McSweeney. He is playing horsie with the little girl. McSweeney is on all fours, the child on his back; he has a leather thong between his teeth, serving as a bridle, and the child is merrily whipping him on his flanks with a loose end of the bridle. Both are naked. The child is Ann Marie Mathison.

I have a few more pictures like that in the head. The play is not always the same and the principals are aging, but they are always naked. I would say that the time span between the frames represents five to six years.

I also have a somewhat foggy image of a typewritten letter on Church of the Light stationery.

I do not have the whole letter but I have the gist.

In it, someone is urging Herman Milhaul to forget about going through with a proposed sex-change operation. Milhaul is also being firmly turned down on a request for $20,000 to pay for the operation. The name McSweeney appears in the text of the letter.

There is another letter—more of a scrawled note—that appears to be an emotional response to the first letter. I do not have the wordage but the intent is clear. It is a threatening letter.

Somehow connected to that scrawled note is an idea of an old .357 Magnum Colt army revolver that once belonged to Tony Mathison, Ann's father.

The rest of what I have, at this point, is a sort of overlay pulling all that together. I believe it to be an overlay provided by Paul Stewart's sensing of the case. A police officer has been arrested and charged with the murder-for-hire of Charles Cohan McSweeney—whether in reality or in Stewart's mental prognosis.

The point of it all, in the police mind, is that McSweeney and Milhaul had been engaged in an extortion plot with Annie the victim. She fought back, but in a method not sanctioned by law.

I had other stuff—all too vague and uncertain to bring out at this point—involving other people in Annie's past.

I will give you just this one little morsel, as a promise of things to come:

Annie's second husband, Donald Huntzermann, had several children from an earlier marriage, all of whom were apparently quite bitter about his marriage to young Ann Mathison. One of these was a daughter, Mildred. Mildred had married a man named Samuel Carver—and that marriage produced a son, David, who grew up to become a cop.

There you go.

Frankly, I did not know where to go with this damned case. It was almost a total confusion in my mind. Where there was not confusion, there was bafflement. What the *hell* was going down, here?

Oh, I had a *sensing,* sure, a *feeling*. But you don't just let yourself leap off to an insane conclusion, not if you can help it. I was trying my damnedest to help it. But I did not know where to go for that help.

So I went back to the Center of Light, which was deserted, and I sat in the gazebo for a while studying my notes on the tutorial that had come down during my earlier visit.

Think I told you that I used to do some work in cryptography. Analytical cryptography demands a pretty good understanding of semantics. In logic, semantics is a study of the relation between signs and symbols and their meanings. In linguistics, it is a study of the meanings of speech forms, and particularly with regard to the evolution of language.

Cryptography today, as it is practiced by the various world governments, is largely done by machine. But a lot of that stuff is doubly encoded. You break a code with your machinery, for example, and get a message that reads, "The cock crows thrice." So what the hell does that mean? This is where the analyst comes in, and he'd better have a good semantic feel for language and lingual symbology.

Semantic decipherment involves quite a bit more than just scrambling words around to find the meaning of a phrase. I mean, don't go in to your boss and tell him that the solution to the cipher is "the crows have three cocks." You would be closer to the truth of this particular cipher if you began to wonder who was disclaiming whom—or if the message really had something to do with the passage of three sunrises—perhaps an instruction to take some action at the third sunrise. But you have to know the context.

I did not pick that example from thin air. I did solve an actual cipher a few years back that was a play on the New Testament story of Jesus before the betrayal at Gethsemane when he foretold that Peter would deny him "thrice" before the cock crowed. You try to consider the words as elements that play against each other and toward each other. In my little example, above, the fully deciphered message could be ordering a terrorist attack upon some preselected Christian target in the Mideast. But you do consider the context.

Context is all-important, in fact. If the *cock crows* double cipher had been intercepted on its way to a Russian sub operating beneath the polar ice, the symbology could be very puzzling. I would have to pull the file on that Russian skipper and try to understand why he'd been doubled with that particular phrase instead of a hammer striking an anvil or something to do with the victory of the working class.

So I knew that I was working out of my own depth with this message from another world—if that, indeed, is what it was. I had not yet decided what the hell it was or that it meant anything beyond warmed-over bromides served up purely for my bedazzlement. But I had to reach for something and that was all I had, at the moment.

So I took "peril precedes peace" and read that as simply a setup, a prefacing statement, like "be careful."

Then we had "sorrow accompanies joy." That could simply mean that you pay for what you get: be prepared to pay.

Next was "strangers become lovers" and "lovers become strangers." Nothing is forever, all is in flux, be prepared to drop old alliances and forge new ones.

How about "the virgin lusts while the satyr rests?" There's a goodie. I passed, for the moment.

"Authority corrupts compassion" means exactly what it says. Someone—need we ask who?— is in for a hard time with the people in charge of justice.

"Dispersion feeds reversion." That's almost a homily. It's like the major fear of ethnic groups who want to preserve their culture. Or, perhaps more in context, you take a band of savages and make Christians of them. Long as you keep them all together, they'll probably remain good Christians. It's like peer support. Let them start drifting away, though— dispersing—and they will go back to their old habits of eating the missionaries.

"Community bests disunity" could mean about the same thing except for the choice of "bests" instead of "beats." We get here a feeling of disunity being overthrown by an organized attempt to bring everybody together. Read these two together as a single statement for the best understanding.

The next two are definitely a pair; they even rhyme. "Flesh decays when the spirit weeps; Life delays what the devil reaps." This reminded me of a line from the eighteenth-century poet, Christopher Smart: "For he counteracts the Devil, who is Death, by brisking about the life."

But I am reserving this one, too, because something biblical is at the tip of my tongue and won't get on.

The rest of it seemed fairly obvious, but I still decided I was wasting my time on this stuff. I simply did not have the deep context, nor even an understanding of what the tutorials in general were supposed to do. Janulski had hinted that they were some sort of heavenly revelation fraught with significance. I withheld judgment on that idea, too. I would have loved to see an official translation. But that was not in the cards, either, because the whole place was locked up tight and a notice on the bulletin board by the gazebo announced the cancellation of all scheduled activities until further notice.

So I put the notes away and broke into the joint.

And I very quickly wished that I had not done that.

The general offices were in quiet bedlam. If that sounds like a contradiction of terms then you just do not understand how loud quiet can get in the spirit world.

A seance or whatever was in progress in the reception area. I guess they were doing it there because it was the only room large enough to contain it. Twelve people were scattered about on leather couches and chairs, each a channel, and microphones had been carefully placed to record each precious whisper.

Except that you really cannot call that sound whispering. Sibilant, yes, but harshly so, and all mixed together from the twelve mouths all moving at once yet integrated somehow so that no two spoke at precisely the same moment. But the flow—the *flow*—like water over a dam was unbroken, an endless phonetic sigh emanating from twelve separate sources to produce a single flow. But it did not sound like a flow. It sounded like bedlam, and it was bedlam.

Other people were up and moving hurriedly about through all that, to and fro between the other offices and along the corridor to an inner courtyard, like the seemingly confused frenzy of ants at a picnic, moving files and records outside and dumping them in a common pile. Must have been twenty people in all, counting the séance mediums, and Bruce Janulski was one of those on the move.

He walked past me twice without acknowledging my presence—without even seeing me, I believe. I thought about putting an arm on him his second time through but decided against it. He was like a man in trance, moving with a single purpose.

None of them noticed me, except to step around me when I got in the way. I saw Ted, the medium, except he was not mediuming at the moment—he was one of the ants—and I recognized one of the office ladies, but I was really all alone with myself in that nuthouse.

So I wandered on through to the courtyard and checked out the growing pile of papers. Hell, it looked like financial records, computer printouts of membership rolls or something, ream after ream of writings—probably tutorials—stacks of correspondence, inventories—anything and everything relating to the activities of this organization.

These people were getting ready for a bonfire!

I swiped a few pages from a stack of tutorials and went on through to the other side of the complex, into the auditorium which officially served as the church facility.

There was nobody in there but I was following a hunch, went on to the room behind the stage.

Annie was "there," yeah. Naked, standing in the same shaft of light, arms upraised in that same pose.

But she was not the only one.

The other three spotlights were shining, too, and their beams were occupied by three more dazzlingly naked females.

One of those was the busty Rachel who had channeled for me earlier. The big tits were not her only attributes, let me tell you.

I did not recognize the other two—but of course I had never seen them in that particular light before, so maybe . . .

They were all sizzling.

I just stood there frozen for maybe thirty seconds.

And then Annie very slowly abandoned her pose and turned to look at me. Our eyes joined and I swear something in me fused to something in her.

She gave me a beatific smile and said to me, "I knew you'd come."

I think I went a little crazy there, then, because the next really coherent memory I have of that experience finds me standing naked, also; the beams have merged into a single shaft of light and we all share it; my arms are raised in that same pose with all the girls and I am at the center; their bodies are gripping mine like a hot dog bun surrounding a wiener; and that, pal, was the very end of coherence.

CHAPTER
TWENTY-SEVEN

A Relative Objectivity

I was falling through a shaft of light that seemed endless. I did some skydiving once and that is the closest experience I can relate it to—the freefall stage—but this was freefall with no restricting medium, like falling through a vacuum, absolute zero gravity; and it was pleasant, very pleasant. Annie and I were embracing. I adored her and she adored me; the surge of complementing emotions was almost overpowering, like I wanted to laugh and cry all at once. Yet it was not like hysteria; it was sweet and good. I was peakingly aware but the peak never decayed; it just hung there, sharp and wonderful. I could feel her heart beating against my chest and I could feel her hair on my face and taste it and smell it; I was stunningly aware of her flesh on my flesh, the soft little belly warm against mine, legs restlessly intertwined, hands caressing hands and faces and shoulders. But it was her eyes that were absolutely tearing me up, eyes deeper than all the reaches of space and pouring love from all those depths; and I knew for the first time what love can really be; love is where it's at and what it is and the reason for all the reasons.

"We shall meet again; we shall fall in love."

At such a moment, I thought of that—and I understood it and accepted it. We had met again and we were falling, in love.

I understood something about love, too, in that moment. It is an ever-seeking force, and it seeks itself. At this moment it had found itself and I was exultantly participating in that discovery.

But there was a problem. A problem, of sorts. I was fully extended in all my dimensions, and sexuality is one of those; my sexual extension was at infinite limit; immersed in all that sweet and tender and understanding love, I was also at the same moment an infinitely swollen penis shaking with the frenzied need for union, and that was the problem. Recognition of the problem added another dimension to my understanding of love; love without sex is a postponement of love's fulfilling power, a diversion or scattering of the force. It added also to my understanding of sex without love; sex without love is the consolation sought by the scattered pieces.

I said to Annie, "There is too much sex without love because there is too much love without sex."

And Annie replied to me, almost whimpering with sweet stress, "Yes, but please be patient with me. I am trying."

She was trying, yes, but without notable success. My sexual extension was about to burst.

We kept falling through nothingness and Annie kept trying. Suddenly she stiffened against me, inhaled sharply; said, "Ohhh. Yes. Ohhhhh."

And I really understood, then, what love truly is.

I was in a very different place. Different from what, I don't know; just different; no, very different. There was no up or down, no side to side, no depth extension. Yet there was no lack of any of that, either.

I puzzled about that for a moment and then I realized that what was lacking was relativity. There was no relativity.

There was an up but it was the same as down; a side but the same as the other side; a depth but all was depth.

I thought of Lewis Carroll, then, and wondered where that guy had gone to get Alice's adventures in Wonderland. A place like this? Did a place like this exist in 1865? Or did 1865 forever exist in a place like this?

Mr. Lincoln? Are you there?

He was not, but another was.

Dear old Dad was there. I was not really sure that I was; but he was. He was the whole place, I think. I mean, he was everywhere there.

I asked him, "What is this place?"

He asked me, "What would you like it to be?"

I said, "Is it as easy as that?"

He said, "It's as easy as you want to make it."

I asked, "Is that good?"

He replied, "Is it bad?"

I told him, "Hell, I don't know. Isn't it the same thing?"

He chuckled and told me, "You're the boss. It's what you make it."

I asked, "What is?"

He replied, "Everything is."

I snapped my fingers, I think, or I snapped something and said, "Like this?"

He smiled and said, "Sure."

I said, "Are you really my dad?"

He said, "Yes. But also your son."

I said, "Wait right there. You have to be one or the other."

He said, "I am."

I said, "You are? Okay. Which one?"

He said, "Of course."

I thought, shit, I'm in heaven with a comedian.

But he heard that thought and he laughed and told me, "If that's the way you want it, that's fine with me."

I said, "My will be done?"

He said, "Always."

I had to think about that. Finally I told him, "I think I need some relativity."

He said, "Okay."

"Objectivity."

"Okay."

"Where the hell am I?"

"You are at home."

"At home?"

"Relatively, yes."

"How about objectively?"

"Objectively you are between there and there. Or here and here. However you prefer it."

I said, "I just want to know what the hell is going down."

He replied, "That is in review."

"What do you mean by *in review*?"

"Relatively or objectively?"

"Both."

He chuckled; told me, "The antecedent follows the precedent."

I said, "Don't give me fucking tutorials."

So he said, "That which may be usually follows that which has been."

I wanted to argue about that. I said, "That sounds like bullshit. Tell it to Darwin. If that which was governs that which is or may be, then where is change?"

He showed me a patient and tolerant smile. "You forget fruition."

"The cosmic egg," I decided.

He gave me a delighted smile. "Exactly."

"So what is in review?"

"A route."

"A route? A route is in review?"

"Yes."

"Route to where?"

"Route to there," he said enigmatically.

"Where is there?"

He said, "Exactly. We might have to intervene."

"Intervene?"

He replied, "Yes. Scrub the route, you know."

"Abort it? Abort the mission?"

He said, "You could put it that way, yes."

My head was beginning to hurt. Or something was. I told him, "This is all very confusing."

He told me, "If you demand relativity and objectivity, how could it be otherwise?"

I told him; getting angry, now, "You are telling me that relativity and objectivity are the source of confusion."

He replied, "And the mother of invention."

I said, "You mean necessity."

He said, "There is no necessity except in confusion."

"That's pure baloney!" I argued.

"Relatively and objectively," he replied, "you're something of an arrogant bastard, aren't you."

I growled, "Thanks, Dad. Maybe I come by it naturally."

He chuckled, said, "Yes, your mother always had that problem."

"Comedians," I complained. "Heaven is filled with comedians."

"How else could we bear you?" he replied to that.

I laughed and he laughed.

I said, 'bye and he said 'bye.

And then I awakened in Rachel's arms.

And Rachel was dead.

The other girls were dead, too. Annie was not there, of course; had not been there, not really, not all of Annie.

I could find no marks on the bodies, no visible evidence of the cause of death.

There was evidence of a different kind on me, though, drying little puddles of semen streaked across both thighs. I staggered into the little bathroom and washed that off, then quickly got into my clothes. There was a smell in the air, in there, a disturbing smell, and I think I knew what it was even before I got outside.

I was stunned and confused and sad and exalted all at once and I barely knew my own name but I knew smoke when I smelled it and I knew what it meant. Reality was crashing in on me and I was remembering the bonfire fuel in the courtyard.

Two of the surrounding roofs were blazing when I got there, and the entire courtyard was intensely hot. Ted was lying curled on his side near the door to the office corridor; another guy was a few yards away; both were dead but they were not burned and really looked quite relaxed in their death, the same as the girls back there, as though it had come to them easily.

I found a garden hose and turned it on but the pressure was not all that great; it was like pissing into the wind. I heard distant sirens, though, and knew they were coming my way, so I threw the hose down and ran into the general offices.

It was hot in there but not blazing yet. But, God, there was death; bodies strewn everywhere; I hoped it was a nightmare but knew it was not.

Those folks had all died easy, some just reclining back onto the couches; others toppled from their chairs; a couple of men holding hands and sprawled across the corridor.

I could not find Janulski; he was not among those dead.

I found the recording equipment in a small vaultlike room behind his office. It had all been turned off and the tapes removed. Specially designed tape storage cabinets lining the walls stood bare with doors agape.

I ran through the offices like a crazy man, trying to find something alive, but finally had to give it up and get the hell out of there. The walls had become so hot they could spontaneously ignite at any moment.

The firemen were there and going through their preliminary drill. I grabbed one with captain's bars and told him where the bodies were. He jerked his head in an understanding nod and sent his troops into the battle.

I had just emerged from that war zone so knew where they were headed, and I had to respect those guys . . . but I could not help them and I was just in the way. So I went on to the parking lot and found the Maserati and moved it safely to the rear then tried the mobile phone and connected with Paul Stewart.

I told him what had happened—well, most of it—but that took awhile because I had to repeat myself a lot; guess I was not speaking too clearly. My chest hurt and my head hurt and I was all but overwhelmed by an ever-deepening sadness.

I do not remember ending that telephone conversation.

I just remember sitting there in the Maserati watching the smoke billowing up from the Spiritual Center of Light and trying to remember what had led up to this.

That is where I was and the way I was when Stewart opened the door and slid in beside me.

"You okay?" he asked gruffly.

I assured him that I was—but hell I really did not know if I was or not.

He said, tautly, "They got all the bodies out."

I said, quietly, "That's nice."

He said, "First look says they were dead before the fire."

I replied, "Yes, I think that is probably correct."

He asked, "What's been going on here?"

I told him, "Beats the shit out of me, Paul."

He said, "You don't know?"

I said, "Right. I don't know."

He said, "If you find out, will you tell me?"

I told him, "Hell, you're the cop."

He said, "Looks like another Jonestown."

I asked him, "Another what?"

"That religious cult that all killed themselves back in '78, the Jim Jones bunch. Another one of those."

I said, "Oh, shit."

He said, "Yeah. Numbs the mind, doesn't it."

I said, "Tell me about it."

He said, "I'll tell you about your friend Annie. I had just been on the horn with the jailer when you called me. She's had a little problem. A strange little problem."

I should have been prepared for it but I was just sitting there mostly stunned and stupid. I said, "What strange little problem?"

"Had to rush her to the infirmary. Had a hemorrhage."

"Had what?"

"Hemorrhage. They thought at first it was from the vagina. Turned out to be not quite that."

"What do you mean, not quite?"

He said, "It's baffling. Don't know what to make of it."

I was losing the stuns, I guess. I said, "Let's both be baffled. What the hell are you talking about?"

"Wasn't exactly vaginal. It was virginal."

I repeated, stupid again, "Virginal?"

"Yeah. Can you beat it? Thirty-five years old. Married four times. But the jail doctor says her hymen not only was still intact, but it was so extensive and so tough before the rupture that there is just no way that lady could have ever got laid. She would have needed surgery first. Can you buy that?"

I'd already bought it.

I was remembering a dream. Or whatever the hell it was.

I heard myself asking Stewart in a dull voice, "It ruptured, huh?"

He replied, "Well not spontaneously, no. She obviously had a little help."

"A little help," I echoed.

"Or else she helped herself. Just can't figure out why."

I sighed, and knew why.

I just did not know why all those people had to die, in the bargain.

CHAPTER TWENTY-EIGHT

Tutorial on the Mountain

Sigmund Freud once remarked that religion is the most incurable form of insanity.

Freud was pure atheist, I guess, so I'm sure he was thinking of the entire religious instinct.

Of course, who really knows what insanity really is?

Maybe you could turn it around and say that insanity is the strongest form of religious expression.

Nobody really knows what insanity is. Even Freud, for all his acknowledged genius, was just a man; subject, therefore, to error the same as all men.

North American Indians revered the insane. Most Europeans, I guess, have always abhorred them. They locked up their lunatics and threw away the keys, abused them terribly; maybe they were really just terribly frightened and insecure about the whole thing.

Nobody really knows what it is all about. Certainly the crazy people live in a reality quite different from the common reality. That makes them a minority; it does not necessarily make them wrong within their own minority except as they wrong themselves. Maybe insanity is an entirely natural state of being, for those who are there. Maybe these folks just have a different window onto reality and find it too difficult to adjust to ours. Maybe all the electric shocks and drugs and other therapies can convert them to our view— but does that not also give them an unnatural window if it can be maintained only in that way?

I know; I rationalize. I propose while God disposes. But shit, that is what my head is for. Isn't it? Isn't that what yours is for, too?

But, you see—I am thinking . . . maybe I am crazy, too. I am thinking, maybe the psychic sense is just another form of mental derangement. None of that shit really happened. I dreamed it up. I went into some kind of asshole trance and fantasized a sexual experience with a woman who all the while was locked up across town, and I frolicked in my insanity while a dream burned and folks died all around me.

Dear old Dad is no more than a fantasy extension of my own insanity, a delusion fed by rampant neurones out of place in space and time, out of touch with reality and monstrously out of context with that which is noble and good.

I am thinking that, yes, but all the while I am thinking it I know this is bullshit. I did make love with Annie, or with some beautifully tangible essense of Annie, and I did have a genuine mystical experience.

If that is insanity, then I'll take it.

But don't ask how Annie projected herself from that jail cell into the sanctuary and that beam of light. Hell. I have had many out-of-body experiences myself, and I don't know how *I* do that. If we had to understand everything before we did it we'd all drop dead because nobody knows consciously how to make his own heart beat. It just does, and we go with it. Out-of-body, too.

But if you need some official documentation, there does exist quite a bit of covering literature. Look it up. Wouldn't hurt you. Such as the case of Alphonse de Liguori. He was the founder of an eighteenth-century Christian monastic order. In the year 1774, this monk who was later canonized fell into a trance while fasting in his monastery which was located four days travel from Rome. He came out of the trance to announce the death of Pope Clement XIV and claimed to have been at his deathbed. It was later confirmed by others who attended the pope's final hours that Liguori indeed had been present, that he had spoken to them, and that he had assisted in the last rites for the pope. So go figure it.

Of course this stuff is not reserved for religious professionals—but I do think a certain religious orientation is required before it can happen. John Donne, for example, the seventeenth-century poet who gave us, among many other beautiful things, "send not to ask for whom the bell tolls; it tolls for thee," reported seeing in Paris a wraith of his wife carrying a dead child within the same hour that his wife in London delivered a stillborn son.

Similar experiences are mentioned by such as Lincoln, Goethe, and Shelley in which the "wraith" is the observer's own double.

All of the cases recorded in the literature on the subject seem to involve individuals who are otherwise known to possess strong spiritual qualities. Are all such people nuts? If so, we should all be so nuts. It would be a kinder world.

Well, of course, I did not mention any of this to Stewart. He probably would have suspected, anyway, that I dreamed it up just to explain what had happened to Annie in her jail cell.

I did follow him to police headquarters where I dictated a statement and signed the transcript. After that, we sat around and talked for a while.

Like some other cops I've known, Stewart seemed to be married to his work. It was, by now, eight o'clock in the evening and I knew the guy had been there at least since eight that morning.

I had not really known Stewart before this case. I was getting to know him and like him. Another reason why I kept a lot of stuff to myself. It is not too smart to say too much too soon to people who have never really been exposed to this sort of thing. You get a reputation, that way, and it precedes you wherever you go; establishes a bias against you; be advised, if you dabble: do it quietly. Folks loved Annie, sure, but that was because she was discreet. She showed them a few of her lighter tricks, and they loved it. But the whole bag would have scared the shit out of them; they would have said she was nutty instead of gifted, and there would go the ball game.

So when Stewart asked me, point blank, "Is that woman really psychic?"—I replied only that I could validate certain specific instances of strong psychic ability.

He asked, "What was she trying to pull, do you think,

doing something like that to herself? Making some kind of statement?"

I looked at my feet and replied, "Maybe. Maybe not."

"Don't give me that," he protested amiably. "It was a stunt, wasn't it. I've heard of these people down in the Philippines, these so-called psychic surgeons, who were caught with their fingers in a bucket of chicken guts. I mean, supposedly they were pulling that shit out of their patients without cutting on them. But it was all rigged. Maybe her, too. Maybe one of the lawyers smuggled something in."

"Something like what?" I inquired mildly. "A chicken's hymen?"

He laughed and said, "Well, I don't know how she did it. That's why I'm asking you."

I showed him my hands. "Women have been working that con since Eve, haven't they. I don't know how they do it. Ask one."

He said, "Already did. Asked my wife. She told me this story her grandmother told about a young girl who'd lost her cherry to another guy before her wedding day. She was terrified. It was a big deal, back then. So she managed to delay the wedding until she was on a period. Stuffed her vagina with gauze, screamed like hell when the kid tried to penetrate her, jumped up and ran into the bathroom and removed the gauze behind the locked door. So she had the bloody evidence. And she held the groom off, pleading soreness, until her period was over."

I chuckled and said, "We made them do it, you know. Our fault entirely."

He said, "Sure, but that's not the point. How'd Annie do it?"

I suggested, "More to the point, why would she?"

He frowned; said, "I don't know. And I'm afraid to find out."

I shuffled my feet about for a moment then asked, very offhandedly, "Think it's somehow connected to what happened at the center?"

He replied, "How could she set up something like that? Surely those lawyers wouldn't. . . . And she's been incommunicado except for them. Why would she *do* something like that?"

I said, "Maybe you're reaching too far. We don't know yet why the center staff did that to themselves. Maybe we should wait until the facts are in."

"Yeah," he said quietly. "We don't even know *if* they did it to themselves." He glanced at the clock. "Christ, we should be getting the autopsy results by now. What the hell are those people doing? Don't they know that all the eleven o'clock news people back East are dying to hear?"

I suggested, "The coroner is going to be very careful on this, Paul. We could get nothing 'til morning. So why don't you go home and strike up an acquaintance with your wife and kids?"

He looked at the floor and said, "They can't take me at a time like this."

I said, "Or you can't take them?"

"Either way," he said, "it's the same thing."

"Not exactly," I said, and told him good night.

I had to get out of there. Cops all over the L.A. area were searching for Bruce Janulski. I wanted to search, too. And I had a better way.

* * *

I was beginning to get my head back together after the stunning events at the Center of Light, and the realization came that I was a bit smarter than before. In fact, I had developed my theory of the case by the time I left Paul Stewart's office that night.

Before I say more about that, though, I need to be certain that you are with me in this matter of the so-called masters' game. We are talking reincarnation, of course, but consider what I have to say before you make up your mind as to how you want to feel about that. There are, it seems, almost as many reincarnation theorys as theorists in the Western world —so let's just make sure we understand the terms.

Most people raised in the Christian faith have little if any understanding of these ideas; most who now embrace Christianity will have nothing to do with these lunatic ideas.

It is true that the metaphysical system which is now in place as Christianity admits no debt to reincarnationist theories, except a belief in some Christian quarters that all the saved souls will rise from their graves and be restored at the day of judgment. There is considerable and persistent dichotomy in this particular area, however, and therefore considerable confusion among many devout Christians as to just what Jesus has in mind for them when they die. This is due chiefly to the fact that Jesus himself was not a Christian and would not understand, either, the new metaphysics that are supposedly based on his teachings.

Jesus was a Jew. He was a very devout Jew and obviously well educated into the liturgies and the traditions of Israel. I believe that he was also a psychic, or—at the very least— particularly sensitive to the needs and aspirations of his own people. He was also a hell of a logician, and his command of semantic symbology was positively brilliant. How better get the attention of hardworking fishermen intent at drying and repairing their nets on a hot Mideastern day than to suggest to them, "I will make you fishers of men." And how much cooler and quieter win the confidence of a frightened woman outside the gates of a remote village, surprised by male strangers as she labors to draw water from the well which then must be carried upon the shoulder all the way home (and how many tiring trips each day?), than to promise that woman, "I can give you living water."

He had their rhythms, see, and he had their moods. He knew who they were and where their heads were because he was one of them and because he was smarter than most.

And because he believed the traditions.

He knew who he was; he knew who they were; and he had a sensing of his own destiny.

And maybe a whole lot more.

In Luke 9, the story of the transfiguration, he had gone to the mountain with three disciples to pray. As Jesus was praying, the others saw that "the appearance of his countenance was altered, and his raiment became dazzling white. And behold, two men talked with him, Moses and Elijah, who appeared in glory and spoke of his departure, which he was to accomplish at Jerusalem."

Moses and Elijah were, of course, greatly revered teachers in the Jewish tradition—but both had died centuries before. The phrase *appeared in glory* is typically used in scripture to describe a Godly or angelic manifestation. The "departure" at Jerusalem refers, of course, to the death of Jesus. "Which he was to accomplish" speaks, I think, for itself. This was a strategy session.

The very next day, Jesus gathered his disciples and said to

them, "Let these words sink into your ears; for the Son of man is to be delivered into the hands of men."

It is later reported, in that same chapter of Luke, that "when the days drew near for him to be received up, he set his face to go to Jerusalem."

The same story, in Matthew 17, tells an important detail that for some reason did not survive in the Luke narrative. As they are coming down the mountain after the meeting with Moses and Elijah, Jesus commanded the three disciples who witnessed that to say nothing of the vision "until the Son of man is raised from the dead."

One of the disciples then asked Jesus, "Then why do the scribes say that first Elijah must come?"

Jesus replied, "Elijah does come, and he is to restore all things; but I tell you that Elijah has already come, and they did not know him, but did to him whatever they pleased. So also the Son of man will suffer at their hands."

Matthew then tells us: "Then the disciples understood that he was speaking to them of John the Baptist."

Is this a masters' game or not? If Elijah returned as John the Baptist, is this a reincarnation or not?

As a matter of fact, all devout Jews of the period believed that their prophets returned in life after life to guide them. The conference on the mountaintop among Jesus, Moses, and Elijah is not at all startling in Jewish tradition. This was an entirely normative transaction in the lives of the prophets.

And now the entire Christian edifice is built upon the proposition that Jesus entered Jerusalem with every expectation of dying there and being lifted up to heaven; furthermore, he was careful to follow the tradition, even as to his entry into the city (Matthew 21):"This took place to fulfill what was spoken by the prophet, saying,

"Tell the daughter of Zion,
'Behold, your king is coming to you,
humble, and mounted on an ass,
and on a colt, the foal of an ass.'

"The disciples went and did as Jesus had directed them."
Nobody ever said that a masters' game was an easy one.
But sometimes it's the only game in town.

CHAPTER TWENTY-NINE

Game of Masters

Remember the trouble I'd had breaking the tutorial? Well it had all come together somewhere down inside the labyrinths of mind, maybe after bumping against the stuff I'd filched from Paul Stewart earlier and the conversation with Dear old Dad after my phantom cavorting with Annie. I checked the context with the fragments of older records picked off the bonfire pile before the destruction of the center, and I am entirely satisfied in my own mind that I have reconstructed the message as it was intended to be understood.

Before I give you that, though, here is the other stuff I promised you when I told you about Carver's connection to Annie via Donald Huntzermann, who was Carver's maternal grandfather. It is rather intricate and amazing stuff, but try to keep in mind the game that we are tracking here. Don't bother about trying to unscramble these relationships; just remember that they exist.

Charles McSweeney was a first cousin to Annie's late father, Tony Mathison, so second cousin to Annie.

Herman Milhaul, sometimes also known as Esther, was distantly related to McSweeney and had figured in a molestation charge when Herman was ten years old. He testified to a relationship spanning several years but later recanted and the case against McSweeney was dropped. Some sort of relationship evidently continued through the years because Milhaul worked at the film lab that was involved in processing and copying McSweeney's old 16mm film that figured in the kiddie porn case still pending against McSweeney at the time of his death.

Herman was also Clara Boone's nephew. Both he and McSweeney were occasional participants in Clara's past-lives study group.

Now Clara's half-sister, Mary, the silent film star, is the mother of Annie's first husband, Nathan, which means that Ann was briefly related by marriage to Herman—but look out for this one—Herman's mother, and I have no idea what her name is (nor do I wish to know)—Herman's mother was Nathan's father's sister, so that makes Wayne Sturgis the uncle of Herman Milhaul and therefore related by one device or another to McSweeney.

But I am not finished with this.

Clara Boone's brother (whom we have not and will not meet here) was married to Maizey McCall before Maizey was married to Tony Mathison, Ann's father. And Tony Mathison, believe it or not, was married to Clara's sister,

Mary—Wayne Sturgis's present wife—when Tony met Maizey. (Which could explain why the sisters were estranged all those years; Maizey and Clara were good buddies.)

Got all that?

Okay, here's some more. Donald Huntzermann, Annie's second husband, had been married briefly to Wayne Sturgis's sister, Herman Milhaul's mother. And Milhaul's natural father had been killed in a traffic accident involving George Farrel, Ann's fourth and latest husband, when Milhaul was only two years old.

And, of course, Farrel was Bruce Janulski's natural father.

That brings us to Larry Preston, Annie's third husband, the dry cleaner whose truck exploded on a freeway. Ready? Larry's first wife was Charlie McSweeney's sister.

Is it any wonder that David Carver was half crazy trying to unravel this thing, especially since we already know that Annie's second husband was his grandfather, which makes Annie his step-grandmother, and I hope you caught the connection with Milhaul: Carver's grandfather had briefly been Milhaul's stepfather.

One small item here: Carver's mother also is a member of the past-lives group involving Clara, Milhaul, and McSweeney.

And a final tidbit that may mean nothing whatever but I toss it in merely to round out the picture. Janulski's mother was a sixteen-year-old named Mary Magdalene who died shortly after his birth.

So there's our cast of players. Have you noticed the string of names that begin with the letter *M*? It's probably no more than a curiosity . . . the same as another interesting string

I've noted—John, James, Judas, Jesus, Jerusalem, Jehovah . . .

And so what do you make of our game, at this point?

Keep in mind, before you leap, what I said earlier about the two patterns of death: the one preceding Annie's apparent state of independence and the one since.

And please remember something that my dear old dad said to me: the antecedent follows the precedent. Has something to do with fruition, I believe.

Here is the translation of the tutorial, with a dash of synthesis to tie it all together:

"There is extreme danger if you persist in the present activity."

"You have been warned of the high price to pay if you lose the disciplines."

"Now you have lost all discipline. The group is no longer the group."

"Your project grows desperate and the leaders without the will to lead."

"You are now under relentless attack, and they will not deal kindly with you."

"You must stop the outward flow and reconcentrate the energies if you intend to persist."

"Otherwise all is death and the game is lost."

"You must follow the leader, and the leader must follow the disciplines."

"The leader is the disciplines, and the disciplines must lead."

"Otherwise, we see failure."

"The entire world will rise up to refute you."

"You have lost the object of the game yet you think that you have found it."

"That which you now desire will destroy you."

"Return to the disciplines."

"Beware of foolish behavior."

"Remain firm in your game!"

"Get out of Hollywood!"

"Sever all ties that seek to use you for personal gain!"

There you go. In a nutshell, this was a warning that everything was going to hell. The work of years (or maybe centuries!) was in jeopardy because of a sudden loss of direction. Only a quick and decisive turnaround could save the game. And apparently François Mirabel and his plans for Annie were at the root of all the trouble. But I detected a note of something else, too, and I needed time to think about that.

Problem was, all the time had run out, it seems, and this route had already been scrubbed.

But I still wanted to know why.

I hesitate to mention it because already I have dwelt too long with the Jesus story, but this whole thing gave a new poignancy to that story. It provides a very personal look at the inside drama involving the fruition at Jerusalem as Jesus considered his fate in the garden at Gethsemane. I think he wanted out.

Let's pick it up at Matthew 36:

> Then Jesus went with them to a place called
> Gethsemane, and he said to the disciples, "Sit
> here, while I go yonder and pray." And
> taking with him Peter and the two sons of
> Zebedee, he began to be sorrowful and
> troubled. Then he said to them, "My soul is
> very sorrowful, even to death; remain here,

and watch with me." And going a little farther
he fell on his face and prayed, "My Father, if
it be possible, let this cup pass from me;
nevertheless, not as I will, but as thou wilt."
And he came to the disciples and found them
sleeping; and he said to Peter, "So, could you
not watch with me one hour? Watch and pray
that you may not enter into temptation; the
spirit indeed is willing, but the flesh is
weak."

Jesus then returned and prayed again, "My Father, if this
cannot pass unless I drink it, thy will be done."

He went back and found the disciples again asleep, so he
returned and prayed a third time, "saying the same words."

Apparently he finally got his answer, because it is written,
Matthew 45:

Then he came to the disciples and said to them, "Are
you still sleeping and taking your rest? Behold, the
hour is at hand, and the Son of man is betrayed into the
hands of sinners. Rise, let us be going; see, my betrayer
is at hand."

The cup would not pass, so Jesus accepted it, steeled
himself, and went out to fulfill his destiny. I think he was a
hell of a man.

By and large, I think, the masters come at us with no games
at all. They come quietly to enlighten, to lead, to inspire.
They might come via music or literature, science or industry,

even politics and the military, sometimes through religion.

But when they come with a game, it is because things have become a bit desperate on earth. And the games, when successful, always move the earth—though perhaps not always in a direction which we with the earthbound view would call delightful.

The setup, as I understand it, can take generations to put into place. A theater must first be chosen and the stage prepared. A script must be developed, actors selected and all the roles cast. There must be the "wayshowers" like John the Baptist and the villains like Herod and Caiphus, the loyalists like Peter and the traitors like Judas. And finally, of course, there must be a star: the master himself or herself, and this master must have the depth to carry the role. At special times, more than one master.

As I see it, the games are most often designed to irritate and arouse. They are goads, and we—you and me—are the goadees.

I still did not know the name of Annie's game.

But my father in heaven had told me: "You're the boss. It's what you make it."

I would have to see about that.

CHAPTER
THIRTY

The Man

Before I even got out of the building, I knew that I had to talk to Annie. I returned to Stewart's office and told him that.

The cop fixed me with a troubled gaze and said, "Just when I thought we were getting to be friends."

I told him, "Has nothing to do with friendship. I'm not on anybody's fee right now. I want the same thing you want; the truth. I believe I am only one step away from it. Let me talk to her."

He seemed to be considering the request as he replied, "The D.A. probably would not like that."

I suggested, "Okay, so friendship is involved. Or trust. You can fix it. Do it."

"Just one step away, huh?"

"I think so, yeah."

"Maybe if I wired you for sound . . ."

I said, "Or maybe if you pretended to do that."

"What do you mean?"

"I am not going to take a wire in there, Paul. But if the D.A. *thinks* I am . . ."

The cop showed me a thin smile as he replied, "You don't mind asking for anything, do you. Tell me something: why should I do this? If you can give me one word . . ."

I replied, "I can give you two. David Carver."

Our gazes locked for a very pregnant moment—then he sighed and reached for the telephone. "I will have to wire you. You do what you think you have to do with it after you get in there."

I knew how to handle that, sure. Wires were my business, once.

Annie had not been informed of the tragedy at her Center of Light. They had moved her to a jail ward at County General following the hemorrhage but she looked okay—a bit pale but otherwise okay. The nurse pulled the curtains to give us the only privacy possible in a room with nine other patients. There was a moment of awkwardness, once we were alone, but that passed rather quickly.

I asked her, "How you doing, kid?"

She replied, "Fine, thanks."

I took her hand and said, "I bring bad news."

But she already had it, deep in the eyes. She said, "I know."

I took a deep breath; said, "They're all dead, Annie."

She closed her eyes for a moment then turned them to the curtain as she opened them. "Then it's over," she whispered.

"Scrubbed," I told her.

"I see."

"What went wrong?"

She continued to eye the curtain. "I'm afraid it has been wrong for a long time."

"Since François?"

"Before that, even."

"Did you set him up?"

She turned the lovely head to look at me, blinked the eyes rapidly several times; asked, "What?"

I said, "Never mind"; showed her a picture from Clara's old album; asked, "Who is this?"

She took the faded snapshot from my hand and glanced at it; handed it back and told me, "She was my mother."

"Recognize the guy?"

"My mother's lover."

"Remember his name?"

"Read my mind," she replied quietly.

I said, "Then you've known all along that François was . . ."

She said, "Of course I've known."

"Now you read my mind," I said.

She looked at me for a long moment then smiled and said, "Of course I know what happened. Why do you think I am in this hospital bed? Didn't I tell you we'd fall in love?"

I chuckled and said, "I didn't know you meant that literally."

The smile faded. She asked me. "When did they die?"

I said, "Very soon after that."

A tear oozed along her cheek. She whispered, "Why?"

I sighed and told her, "Hell I don't know why, Annie. I was hoping you could tell me why."

She replied in a whisper: "It was not written."

I said, "Maybe somebody penciled it in."

She turned back to the curtain; whispered, "Perhaps."

I stood there silently for a moment then asked her, "Why me, Annie?"

She whispered, "Read my mind."

"I don't want to read your mind. I want you to tell me. After all these years and all those husbands . . . why me?"

She looked at me, then, as she replied, "It did not really happen, you know. This flesh is still virgin flesh."

I asked, "Why is that so important?"

She said, "Please leave me alone, now. My spirit weeps."

I said, "I know . . . I know," and pulled the curtain back.

She took my hand and said, "Thank you."

I said, "For what?"

She smiled weakly and said, "Read my mind."

I was reading it, yeah, and it was tearing me up.

I asked, "Where would I find Bruce?"

She whispered, "Golgotha."

I said, "Like that, eh."

"Yes."

"Are you Mary, then?"

She just gave me a sad, sweet smile and turned away from me. So I went out of there and met Paul Stewart in the waiting room.

He asked, "How'd it go?"

I reported, "About the way I expected it to. Now I need to find Golgotha."

He said, "Who the hell is that?"

"It's not a who," I told him. "It's a where. A hill, maybe."

Stewart said, "There's a thousand hills in this town but I never heard of that one."

I thought maybe I had. Yeah, maybe I had.

I figured Arnold Tostermann, the screenwriter, for just the guy to give me a quick answer to a simple question, and I'd figured right. A thirty-second telephone conversation with Tostermann gave me what I needed to know.

I had left the Maserati at the police station and gone with Stewart in his official vehicle to County General. I would need him again in his official capacity to gain entrance to "Golgotha" and I figured it was just as well to have him in on this thing, anyway, so we set off together from the hospital in his car.

There are not a lot of back lots left in Hollywood since the studios began dismantling themselves and selling off their valuable land, but I had remembered one in particular that was still around and there was something vague in the memory about a particular old movie set that had never been demolished. Tostermann confirmed and refined that vague memory and sent us hurtling across town in search of a master gamesman.

Stewart's badge got us through the studio main gate. We left the car at the entrance to the darkened back lot and went the rest of the way on foot.

We found our Golgotha, yeah. Wasn't exactly a hill, after all; just a small mound of earth in a corner of the lot. It was dark back there but not so dark that we could not find our way without artificial lighting; I did not want to use flashlights. There was a muted glow, anyway, from the city lights; the city itself lay just beyond a ten-foot-high wooden fence.

I was not all that sure what I would find there. I did expect to find Janulski . . . but I did not know what else to expect.

Well . . . I should have known.

This was, after all, the only Golgotha in town. And Golgotha was named in the Bible as the place where Jesus was crucified.

The crosses from the old movie set were still in place. They had built them with small platforms placed at the proper height on which the actors could rest their feet while crucified and there was portable scaffolding at the rear to facilitate an easy on and off.

Janulski was up on the middle cross. He had draped a bedsheet or something like that from the crossbar and it was covering him from the neck down.

I cautioned Stewart to remain in the shadows at the bottom of the mound and I went on up alone.

I guess Janulski heard my approach because he called out in a trembly voice, "Who is there?"

I went on to within a few paces from the base of the cross before I stopped and lit a cigarette. I took my time at that; wanted him to get a good look at my face. Then I told him, "Surely you know who is here."

He had a kind of crazy look in his eyes. I could see him perfectly, every feature in clear detail. I guess he could see me okay, too, because he replied, "I knew who you were when first I laid eyes on you."

I said, "That's nice. Who am I, then?"

He warned me, "I have a gun. Don't come any closer."

I had been edging forward when he said that. I glanced back toward the bottom of the mound where I had left Stewart. I could see him, vaguely, and I knew that he could see me even better than I could see him. I just hoped he could hear, as well.

I told Janulski, "You don't need a gun for me, pal. I just came to talk."

"Too late for that," he said emotionally.

I replied, "Yeah. I caught your work at the center. Why'd you have to do that, Bruce?"

He said, "It is over."

I said, "Sure is. For those folks, anyway. Why?"

"It was their choice," he told me.

"So what did they prove?"

"Nothing to prove," he replied. "Something to accomplish."

"What was accomplished, then?"

He wet his lips with his tongue and said, "A quick return. We could yet succeed."

I asked, "Succeed in what?"

He said, "You know what."

I said, "It was your game all the time, wasn't it. Not Annie's game. Your game. Her spotlight but your stage."

"Let it be," he said.

"I can't let it be, pal. Too many people are dead. You know you can't play the game that way. You blew it. What was it? The Mirabel money? Was that so tempting?"

"I lost the way," he said humbly. "Don't rub it in."

"Come down and let's talk about it."

"You know that I cannot come down."

The poor guy was sweating, the face all beaded and dripping with it; I knew that he was under severe stress. And I did not know what was beneath that sheet.

I urged him, "We can do it better than this. Come on down."

"I cannot come down."

"Why did you want McSweeney dead?"

He grimaced. "Pervert! He would pull it all apart. For a sexual thrill. He needed to die. He had to die."

"Herman, too? Herman had to die?"

"Of course he had to die! You know who those two were!"

No, I did not, but I let it pass to ask him, "How'd you game it?"

He smiled, coughed lightly, replied, "Patrolman Malloy was with us."

Malloy, eh? With an M. I glanced again toward Stewart; said to Janulski, "Malloy did not get Herman."

He smiled from the cross. "You did."

I said, "You son of a bitch."

He said, "Be kind."

"I said, "You be kind. Tell me about the other cop, my friend David Carver."

"Not mine," he replied. "Selma did that. They didn't like it, either. They called her home over that."

"Why did she do it?"

"She was afraid for Annie. But Carver was, you see, connected. It was a hideous mistake."

"Why did Maizey have to die?" I asked him. "She was old. How could she hurt you?"

"She lost the way long ago."

I asked, "How long ago?"

He replied, "Very long ago. She and all her followers. They began with us. But she wanted Annie for herself."

"All she wanted was a daughter," I told him. "A natural daughter."

He laughed, choked again, spit something from his mouth; said to me, "Then she went about it the wrong way. Annie was never hers."

I asked, "Whose was she?"

He spat again and said nothing.

So I tried again, "Was she Clara's?"

Those eyes were really getting crazy, now. He said, "Stop this. I know who you are. You're the hit man this time, aren't you. I know that you despise me. And I know why you were sent. You overruled me, didn't you. You killed it."

I told him, "I don't know what the hell you're talking about. But I don't despise you. I pity you. Because you are the one who lost the way. You blew the game again. Who are you? Are you Judas?"

He laughed a hollow laugh. "I was never Judas."

I told him, "You are not going to save the game this way."

He told me, "The game is never lost. The game goes on. Only the players change."

I told him, "Wrong. Only the game changes. The players are never lost. You're going to remember that, when you wake up."

He laughed again, but very weakly. "Am I asleep, then?"

"This time, yes," I told him. "You are asleep. What happened to Annie's husbands?"

He said, "They were carefully selected."

"Baby-sitters?"

"You could say that."

"Were you Peter?"

"Do I look like a Peter?"

I said, "No. You look more like an Esther."

He repeated that weak laugh; spat again; told me, "My mother this time was called Mary Magdalene. Don't you know me, Elijah?"

I said, "You've got it all wrong, pal. I was never Elijah."

He laughed, hung his head, and became very still.

I turned to look at Stewart.

He came slowly up the mound; said to me, "You people are giving me the shivers. I think he passed out. Let's get him down."

But Bruce had not passed out.

Bruce was dead.

Beneath that sheet we found him naked and bleeding from various wounds. He had nailed his feet to the platform. He had nailed one hand to the crossbar and then impaled himself onto the upright with a long carving knife. And obviously he'd done all that quite some time before we arrived on the scene.

A banner draped across the shoulders was inscribed: FREE ANNIE FOR SHE IS WITHOUT SIN.

I do not know who the hell that guy was, life to life. But he'd played his masters' game to the bitter end.

And, even with all the errors, and even with all the confusion over sexual roles, he had died a hell of a man.

EPILOGUE

Casefile Wrap-up

Well, I will leave it to you to fill in your own blanks on this one. Already I have said more than should have been said. Guess I could clear up one important point, though, about this reincarnation stuff. Among the most popular Western theories on the subject is the idea of repeating life after life in company with certain groups with whom the individual has become strongly attached. Within the group, the various individuals take on differing relationships from one life to the next. Your father in this life, for example, could have been your son or brother or best friend in a previous one. To the theorist, this occurs whether or not you happen to believe in it. Ordinarily you would never be aware of these deeper relationships but it is believed in certain quarters that it is possible to become aware and even to remember certain events from past lives. Even certain antagonistic personalities, it is said, return to the stage time after time in an attempt to work out on earth the difficulties between them.

I do not know as much as I would like to know about all that. In the aftermath of this case, even, I feel very much ill at ease with the subject and not really inclined to buy anything yet. As for who I am or was, all I know about myself is that I was named for the car in which I was conceived—and please note that I have not changed my name to Studebaker or Buick.

The trouble with coming to terms, you see, is very evident even in the transcript of this case. I do not feel with any certainty that these people knew any more than I knew. I mean, they were still human beings—not gods or angels—and still had to cope with the human situation. No matter how convinced they may have become, through certain experiences, that they were on some vital mission from the stars or wherever, they still had immense doubts, weaknesses, temptations to stray.

I mean, look at the record—Jesus himself begged that the cup be taken away.

So none of us really know with any certainty what is really going on here on this planet. I have to allow the same for Bruce Janulski and his troops. He had a game going, sure, but how much came from his own misunderstanding and self-delusion? You will have to answer that for yourself. I can tell you that Bruce was really the brains and the moving force behind the Center of Light. I have discovered that Annie is simply too far into the spiritual path to have any business sense at all. If you asked her for a dime, she just might give you a hundred dollars; for a shirt, her whole damned wardrobe. That is what became of all the money she came into from the various marriages—she simply gave it away.

Janulski came along and changed all that. He was the

force behind incorporating as a nonprofit organization and he was the energy that manifested itself in the Center of Light activities. Annie may sit beneath a tree all day and meditate but Bruce was there to keep the tree watered.

As for the game he was playing, or thought he was playing . . . who knows? As I have already suggested here, if it was truly a masters' game at play, something very important had to be at stake—something a hell of a lot more important than the self-aggrandizement of a few playful spirits from that other world. So if it really was a game, what was at stake? What has the world lost if an important game has failed? I would not even suggest an answer to such a question, but I would point out that every prophet since Nostradamus has predicted world-shaking events in store for the turn of this century—which, you may have noted, is not now that far away. To suggest that the human race needs no outside help would sound a little foolish, don't you think? The two powerful nuclear powers are still at standoff and rattling missiles at each other; we continue to systematically poison our atmosphere and our oceans; there is very little peace anywhere; the economic gap is ever-widening between the haves and the have-nots; and ordinary people everywhere seem to be becoming less and less concerned about anything or anybody other than themselves. So you go figure if we could use some help or not.

Well . . . with all that, I am happy to be able to close out this transcript on a happy note. Annie has been out of jail for the past three months and it seems doubtful that she will ever return. She has been getting a lot of favorable press and money has been flying in from around the world for her legal defense fund, but I doubt that she will have to spend much of that. She also has friends in court, now—and I heard just yesterday that the D.A. is going to move for dismissal of charges as soon as some of the furor dies down. Bruce's grandstanding suicide, by the way, did not hurt her a bit in that regard.

She and François have become just friends. She even calls him Uncle Frank again, and he seems quite content with that.

Oh, he got a replacement for Annie for his satellite-TV investment, one of the new young born-again evangelists out of Barnum and Bailey. I am sure he will clean up, just like all the others.

As for Annie . . . well, what can I say? Annie will forever be Annie, I guess, and I am sure she will be adored all the days of her life by a great many people.

And, uh, I was visiting with Dear old Dad just the other day. As a result of that little visit, I've had to take another look at my evaluation of the masters' game.

It is quite possible that—after all was said and done—no matter what Bruce thought he had going or for whatever reason—I think it may just be possible that it was Annie's game, after all, all the time.

My father who is in heaven, or wherever, told me just the other day, you see, that Ann Marie is three months pregnant.

Of course, he has to be wrong about that.

As Annie told me from her hospital bed, it did not happen really; that flesh is still virgin flesh, with or without hymen.

But I have been wondering if there could be such a thing as a spiritual surrogate father. Or would it be, let's see . . . a physical surrogate father for a spiritual mother? Or, let's see, would it be . . . ?

Hell. You go figure it. And have a nice day.